Brognola slammed his fist on the desk

"We're looking at a catastrophe, and I'm not even sure that's the right word. There's already major looting in the city. We've got the National Guard, and hell, I can't even count the number of Army and Marine personnel on the way. There's not enough room in all the area hospitals for the wounded, so the Army is setting up makeshift hospitals in the Virginia countryside."

Bolan watched as his friend wiped the blood off his face. A look of raw determination fired Brognola's eyes. Everyone, including the Oval Office, wanted the same thing: retribution, plain and simple.

The Executioner was ready for the job.

MACK BOLAN ®
The Executioner

DON PENDLETON'S
THE EXECUTIONER®
POINT OF IMPACT

A GOLD EAGLE BOOK FROM
WORLDWIDE®

TORONTO • NEW YORK • LONDON
AMSTERDAM • PARIS • SYDNEY • HAMBURG
STOCKHOLM • ATHENS • TOKYO • MILAN
MADRID • WARSAW • BUDAPEST • AUCKLAND

First edition March 2000
ISBN 0-373-64256-3

Special thanks and acknowledgment to
Dan Schmidt for his contribution to this work.

POINT OF IMPACT

Printed in U.S.A.

A man who is good enough to shed his blood for his country is good enough to be given a square deal afterwards....

—Theodore Roosevelt

The man who is angry on the right grounds and with the right people, and in the right manner and at the right moment and for the right length of time, is to be praised.

—Aristotle

To a soldier the ultimate betrayal is one not by his allies but by his country. Returning home after risking his life should be a celebration, not a condemnation.

—Mack Bolan

THE
MACK BOLAN®
LEGEND

Nothing less than a war could have fashioned the destiny of the man called Mack Bolan. Bolan earned the Executioner title in the jungle hell of Vietnam.

But this soldier also wore another name—Sergeant Mercy. He was so tagged because of the compassion he showed to wounded comrades-in-arms and Vietnamese civilians.

Mack Bolan's second tour of duty ended prematurely when he was given emergency leave to return home and bury his family, victims of the Mob. Then he declared a one-man war against the Mafia.

He confronted the Families head-on from coast to coast, and soon a hope of victory began to appear. But Bolan had broken society's every rule. That same society started gunning for this elusive warrior—to no avail.

So Bolan was offered amnesty to work within the system against terrorism. This time, as an employee of Uncle Sam, Bolan became Colonel John Phoenix. With a command center at Stony Man Farm in Virginia, he and his new allies—Able Team and Phoenix Force—waged relentless war on a new adversary: the KGB.

But when his one true love, April Rose, died at the hands of the Soviet terror machine, Bolan severed all ties with Establishment authority.

Now, after a lengthy lone-wolf struggle and much soul-searching, the Executioner has agreed to enter an "arm's-length" alliance with his government once more, reserving the right to pursue personal missions in his Everlasting War.

1

"The Great Satan is about to feel the full wrath of Allah as He works His will against you through all oppressed Islamic peoples. Be they Syrian, Iraqi, be they Palestinian, Egyptian or Pakistani, the Hour of the Cleansing Fire is upon all you devils who have sought the destruction of Islam through your greed, avarice and bigotry. Praise be to Allah. May the blood of all Americans flow in rivers throughout your corrupt land."

It wasn't the first time Mack Bolan had heard the hate spiel from a Muslim terrorist, and he knew it wouldn't be the last. Only this time the particulars of an enemy agenda were nearly as sketchy as the identity of Abu Khaber.

Bolan squared his shoulders, the hint of a smile ghosting his lips. His windbreaker was open, and he could feel all eyes examining the big .44 Magnum Desert Eagle on his hip. The bulge of his other standard side arm, the Beretta 93-R, showed less noticeably, but it was just as tried and true in the warrior's hands. Indeed, he felt the temperature level rise a few degrees, agitation and nerves were like electricity in the air. Forget the hardware, it was something in his stance, the ice in his blue eyes maybe, that carved a little fear in the hearts around him.

Either way something warned friend and foe alike it was going to get ugly for Khaber and his buddy, Nasir Jabel.

With what little intel he had to go on, but carrying a bad feeling in his gut, the man known as the Executioner was on a midnight call for some Q and A. And he was running out of patience.

The big soldier had ridden straight from Stony Man Farm to this Justice Department safe house off Interstate 66, just outside Manassas, Virginia. He was there on a tip about Khaber, armed with carte blanche from Hal Brognola. And the four special agents from the Justice Department were under the big Fed's standing orders to give Special Agent Mike Belasko their complete cooperation. The bottom line, of course, was no questions asked, even if that meant the agents went deaf, dumb and blind over Bolan's interrogation techniques.

The two suspected terrorists in question were now handcuffed and sitting in wooden chairs in the middle of the living room. They sat ramrod stiff, the look of hate and defiance burning in their eyes.

The two-story farmhouse had been bought at the last minute by Brognola when the snatch of the terrorists at Reagan National Airport had gone down. Since Brognola was not only head honcho at the Justice Department but director of the covert Sensitive Operations run out of Stony Man Farm, and answered only to the President of the United States, there was very little he couldn't do when pressed to act.

Once again hard experience showed the Executioner the best way to deal with a terrorist was the direct hands-on approach. Keep it simple.

"Talk about a change of tune. An hour ago he was just a simple Lebanese businessman. Now he's Islam's answer to Alexander the Great," Bolan stated.

The soldier glanced at Special Agent Phil Tomlin then gave the other three agents a once-over, trying to gauge whether they would go with the program if things got rough. Special Agents Peter Simms, Jack Barkley and Margaret Johns appeared to be seasoned pros to Bolan, all steel and determination, waiting on him to begin the question period. If they kept constitutional rights for the accused close to the heart then they might need to take a long coffee break somewhere else.

"We've been here an hour. We are now sixty minutes and counting closer to the Cleansing Fire. And I assume, looking at this man before me," Khaber growled, a thin smile of contempt on his lips as he stared up at Bolan, "you know who I really am."

Bolan had all the facts as given him by Aaron Kurtzman at Stony Man Farm. Fingerprints, mug shots and background checks had been compiled quick but thorough, as Kurtzman, nicknamed the Bear, linked up with databases to the CIA, Interpol and several other international law enforcement agencies. Unfortunately the more they appeared to know, the more questions were raised.

Bolan addressed the terrorist. "Your real name is Abdul Rafiz. You're an Iranian. You were a former captain in SAVAK, the late shah's secret police. You've been linked to several bombings and assassinations in the Middle East, Europe and North Africa. You were arrested for the possession of narcotics and weapons in France but the charges were mysteriously dropped. You're Mohammed Nassir," he told Jabel, "also ex-SAVAK. You come to us complete with a criminal past, but no time spent in jail, with fingers believed to be deep in all kinds of rotten pies. In other words, gentlemen, I'm cutting to the chase."

"Well," Nassir chuckled, "now that we have the introductions out of the way, perhaps you can tell us why we are being detained, and illegally, I might add."

Tomlin nodded to Bolan. "Nothing in their luggage except a change of clothes and a copy of the Koran. Other than their past arrest records and alleged ties to various terrorist groups in the Middle East, I'd say any lawyer they could find would have these two whisked back to Iran with a free pass and full apologies for the misunderstanding, while we're walking around wiping the egg off our faces."

"I'm sure I'm pointing out the obvious when I ask why the forged passports?" Bolan said, and was treated to a smile from Tomlin. "And why the speech just now from Islam's Alexander the Great?"

Bolan searched the faces of the fanatics and read the arrogance in eyes that were laughing at him. "They didn't fly all the way from Beirut to carry a protest sign in front of the White House."

Rafiz grew more smug by the moment. "So, when can we contact a lawyer and watch you wipe egg off your faces? Perhaps I'll mention this unfortunate incident in some future book-movie deal. I may even decide to portray you in a somewhat generous light. You were merely acting stupid. It's forgivable, given the West's warped view of Muslims."

"That's not happening."

Rafiz turned, arrogantly. "Oh, I see. Now what? You slap us around, hold us without food and water? Perhaps make me piss in my pants?"

"You're former SAVAK," Bolan said. "You know the drill."

"You cowardly sons of whores!" Rafiz spit. "You stand there and treat me with contempt and disrespect. How tough, how smug would you be, American, without your guns and without these handcuffs on me?"

Bolan showed the terrorist a cold smile. "Tomlin, the keys are in my car. Drive it to the barn. Leave the lights on, open the barn doors, lights shining into the barn."

When they were filing out, Bolan stared deeply and angrily into the eyes of the terrorists. Their crimes against humanity had never been proved, but Bolan knew the look of the savage all too well, could smell the stink of innocent blood all over their hands. It was a sixth sense he had acquired. In some ways it was sickening to him, how naturally and easily the knowledge came to him that he was face to face with pure evil.

"You've got a story to tell, I can see it in your eyes," Bolan told Rafiz.

The Iranian shrugged, tapped the side of his head with a finger. "Maybe many stories, maybe much knowledge. You'll be left only wondering."

Bolan's chuckle held all the chill of an Arctic wind. "You see yourself as a smart guy?"

"Oh, I am smart, all right, you American pig," Rafiz said. "Smarter than you. Smart enough to know you can't do a thing to me. You have laws, I have rights. I am untouchable."

"Is that right?" Bolan asked, smiling.

IT STARTED with the Dear John letter.

But a soldier's destiny, that road to victory and glory, he thought, can have roots in the strangest beginnings, the unluckiest or most cruel twists of fate. Who needed love anyway, when a man was solid in himself, knew what he was about, sensed he had a special and unique destiny to fulfill?

For Joe Artillon the road to destiny was long since paved, by more than three decades. Such was the life of the warrior. Love was overrated, killing was not.

In the dark, alone, perched at the edge of the Potomac River and concealed in brush, Artillon grimly reflected on the bitter origins of a past that had led him and his teammates to the present. What they had fought for thirty years ago in a war that most Americans had pretty much forgotten about—if they had ever even cared at all.

If nothing else, the fate of an entire city, perhaps a nation and the world at large, rested squarely on the shoulders of a small army of men who used to fight for God and country.

God and country, huh, Artillon thought. What a load of crap. He had long since decided God was dead, and whatever was left of America now belonged to a mixed bag of self-serving, self-absorbed, self-seeking—self, self, self—whining parasites who wouldn't know a real man if he walked up and slapped them silly. Well, a bunch of warriors were about to take what they wanted from this new America, prove to the parasites, up close and personal, just how damn weak they had become.

He punched a button on the chronometer and checked the illuminated dial. Closing on 2400 hours. Kurchin and Weathers had hit the black water a little more than thirty minutes ago. Outfitted in frogman suits, they carried a waterproof backpack toward Key Bridge, a backpack that held the promise of hell on earth.

Traffic was flying across Key Bridge from Georgetown to Rosslyn, the swish of cars on the GW Parkway above sounding almost right on top of his point of cover. Their rented SUV was parked in a clearing something like a lover's lane, overlooking the Potomac. Hell, each agonizing minute of waiting began to feel like hours.

He searched the river in both directions. No boat traffic at the midnight hour, no roving choppers. But he needed to keep his eyes peeled for river cops or park police just the same. If unforeseen problems cropped up, well, that's what the sound-suppressed Glock in his shoulder holster was for.

The water beneath Key Bridge looked calm, smooth as glass. Kurchin and Weathers would stay submerged, using an illuminated compass and occasionally looking through the special night-vision goggles to guide them through the black, cold waters to the middle pillar. It was a good two hundred-yard swim. At that moment Artillon figured they should be fixing the steel cord around the pillar. Cord and clamps would hold the device in place against the strongest currents, the cable having already been measured down to the exact inch the previous night on underwater recon. The package would stay in place, no doubt, until it was ready to be detonated by remote control.

Artillon had been surprised at how heavy it was, hauling it down the hill while his teammates suited up on the bank, but he'd already seen and hefted the thing in Russia. Seventy-nine pounds, twenty inches in length, eleven inches in diameter, it certainly didn't look like much.

What did they say about looks? He stifled a chuckle.

Their Islamic brothers-in-arms called it the Suitcase from Allah. In the military world it was known as an ADM.

Atomic Demolition Munition.

Whatever it was called it was meant to be used specifically to blow up bridges, roads and railroads during retreat, or cut off enemy supply routes and reinforcements. Because of the massive fallout of the ADM and the fact that it didn't require all the endless variety of activation codes, it could, in fact, be radioactivated or set with a timer. It was listed by the military as a dirty bomb.

As far as Artillon, his teammates and the jihad brothers-in-arms were concerned, it was the cleanest and most beautiful thing on earth. And they had two more ADMs and a little something else—a shock package—on hand.

Maybe it was the darkness, the isolation or the waiting that threw him back to yesteryear. Her face flared to life in his mind, out of nowhere. Melissa. Blond, beautiful, clean and as sweet-smelling as a fresh rose. The fragrance of her skin was alive in his nose, sweet as the first taste of carnal knowledge, but it was skin that now belonged to the touch of another man. His first girl; first sex for both. They had been high-school sweethearts, both of them young and wide-eyed about the future, full of passion and vows to each other, promises of family and children, even as he was drafted into the Army. Then on the day he was leaving something happened, more of a look that passed between them than any parting words. All the fear she had on her face as he swore he would return to her. They would be married, one tour of duty, that was all. It was a lie he told her, and he knew it at the time and suspected she knew exactly where his heart was. Eighteen, kid from a no-name, no-future town in Missouri, he was full of piss and fire, ready to prove something to himself going over there ready to John Wayne it against the VC, the forces of evil.

Dear Joe…

Don't think about it, he told himself. He had been a young stupid kid, full of himself, not knowing what the world was really all about, how a woman, no matter how close he thought they were, needed security, had to know tomorrow was in place, her man there, going the distance for her and her alone.

I've met somebody else. Please understand, I still love you, but I'm afraid…

"Bitch."

"Snap out of it, soldier."

He stood, angry with himself for having nearly drowned in the past. They had materialized like wraiths out of the water, shedding masks and flippers before he was even aware of their presence. He searched their faces, and it took another moment to jar himself out of the past. The eyes and teeth of Weathers seemed to shine like brilliant white light, set in his chiseled ebony face. Kurchin's shaved white dome was a stark contrast, and for a heartbeat Artillon feared they both stood out in the dark.

"It's done?" he asked the frogmen.

"Ready. Let's get the hell out of here, we need to raise the Colonel," Kurchin said.

They were moving back up the hill, searching the darkness around them, their combat senses alive. Then a glitch, the arrival of Murphy's Law that was every soldier's dreaded companion, loomed at the top of the hill. Artillon heard Weathers rasp a vicious curse.

The car was parked close to their SUV. They froze, looking uphill. Squinting hard and using the light of passing vehicles on the parkway, they could see two shadows up front. They were holding each other, pawing away like a couple of dogs in heat. Kids.

A red veil dropped over Artillon's eyes, his heart hammering in his chest.

"Go," Artillon said. "I'll deal with this problem."

He waited while Kurchin and Weathers resumed their climb. They knew what had to be done. It was necessary that no witnesses were left behind, no one who might tell a strange tale to the park police or Arlington cops about two men in frogsuits who had come climbing the hill in the middle of the night.

Drawing his Glock 17 pistol, Artillon took a flashlight and snapped it on. He hit them in the eyes with the beam and heard them cry out in alarm. One look at the blond girl...

For a moment that felt frozen in his mind for all eternity, he believed he saw the face of Melissa, even as the girl spotted the gun in his hand and started to scream.

As if he was pulled by some force beyond his body, Artillon strolled to the passenger door and lifted the gun. He heard the boy scream from some point that sounded a million miles or years away. "No!"

As he squeezed the trigger, the first 9 mm round shattered the window in the girl's face. He stood there, the Glock chugging like some distant bleat in his ears. His finger kept pulling the trigger, his hand guiding itself as he fired, watching their faces and skulls erupt in flying chunks all over the car. He wasn't even aware he'd emptied the entire clip until he felt a hand digging into his shoulder.

"Let's go, man! Hell's wrong with you? Two shots would have done it. Let's go, goddammit!"

He went, unsure of the moment, but knowing what he'd just done and why. It was karma, he thought, his warrior's destiny. Joe Artillon, the stupid kid from a no-name town, had just died, the past eradicated like a bad dream. He felt like a new man, the warrior he knew he would always become.

2

The clock was running. No facts yet, nothing Bolan could pin down, but he could feel it out there, a vulture circling, a runaway train aimed straight at civilization. The executioner needed answers.

Bolan rolled, tall and grim, into the twin beams of light knifing into the barn. With no time to waste, he went to work and launched a foot into Nassir's rear, sending him sprawling to the dirt and hay-littered earth. Before entering the barn, Bolan had Tomlin remove their cuffs. The prisoners were now free to act, and the soldier sincerely hoped intimidation would be his strongest weapon, but he was prepared for anything.

Taking his cue from the big American, Rafiz backpedaled away from Bolan. The Iranian looked uncertain but a glimmer of predatory understanding then lit his eyes as he nodded and chuckled, as if he had the American's play figured.

The Executioner shed his jacket and tossed it toward an empty stall. The soldier gave the makeshift ring a quick look. It was a gloomy place, a few bales of hay, a water trough and a wooden bucket, the stink of dung and decay in his nose.

Bolan felt the eyes of the four agents drilling into the back of his head. He looked over his shoulder, about to address them when Agent Tomlin cleared his throat, and stated, "If you need us, sir..."

"You'll be the first to know."

Dismissed, they trudged off, throwing Bolan wary looks over their shoulders. The soldier waited until the night swallowed them, then turned toward Rafiz and Nassir. Both Iranians were lean and mean, a strange light of fear and arrogance burning in their eyes. Their CIA files claimed they were both fifth-degree black belts, Shotokan masters, in fact. But no man went on to become one of SAVAK's finest without brutal training in hand-to-hand combat. The Executioner himself was no stranger to head-to-head knuckle-dusting. And Bolan sensed they knew the deal here. They were being called to face the music. The soldier was going to get some answers.

Bolan took his Beretta, unleathered the Desert Eagle and pitched both weapons to the ground behind him.

"Let's get one thing straight," Bolan said. "I'm in a very bad mood, particularly because a couple of animals who kill innocent women and children have lied to me. You claim to know something I don't and you're holding back. This is how it's going to work. I ask the questions, you provide the answers. If you don't want to enlighten me, well, if you can make it past me and to my weapons, the doors are open. Clear sailing, no strings."

Bolan was looking at Rafiz, but kept Nassir in the

corner of his eye as he closed the gap to the terrorists. Rafiz was backing up.

Instinct already warned the soldier that Nassir would take the bait first.

Nassir was quick, but the Iranian had no idea, of course, just who he was going after. It was a long and looping right hook aimed at the soldier's temple, Nassir believing he had Bolan off-guard. The Iranian might as well have told Bolan his intention. The Executioner dropped at the knees and felt the knuckles graze his scalp. The Iranian had thrown everything he had behind a fist intended to split the American's skull in two. It left Nassir off-balance, open to the Executioner's counterattack. Bolan punched Nassir just below the ribs, a pile driver that caught his liver. The terrorist hit his knees, eyes bulging and sucking wind, clutching his side as if he'd just been split in two.

One down, but not out.

Rafiz went next, dropping into a forward-leaning stance, his clenched fists held low, knuckles down. Bolan wasn't concerned. The Iranian was going for a snap-kick, the stance telegraphing the foot that lashed out for Bolan's groin. The soldier came down with arms crisscrossed, blocking the Iranian's kick at the forearms. The blow jarred Bolan to the bone, but since he'd called the play the soldier was going the distance, no pain, no gain.

Rafiz looked surprised by Bolan's speed, thrown off long enough for the Executioner to hammer a straight right, dead center into the terrorist's nose.

Bone yielded beneath Bolan's fist, and blood flew into the air.

"Who was the American you were traveling with?" Bolan snarled.

The lights had nearly blinked out in Rafiz's eyes as he shook his head. Pain brought tears to the Iranian's eyes, but he wasn't about to cry because he lacked courage. In the movies, Bolan knew, guys landed repeated crunching blows off each other's noses and mouths, shrugged it off as if they'd only been stung by a bee and started flailing again. In reality, the kind of pain he'd just dished out cleaved the brain in two, then swelled the skull as if it was filling with fire. From there, the fire reached out and scalded every nerve ending in the body, making a man think about nothing except ending the pain.

But this fight was far from over. In fact, Bolan's problems doubled in the next second.

Rafiz leapt to his feet, pulling himself together in a mindless charge of pure rage. Rafiz feinted with a left, then kicked Bolan in the side. White-hot pain knifed Bolan's ribs, nearly doubling him over, but the soldier caught Nassir making his own move and held on. Out of the corner of his eye, Bolan glimpsed Nassir crawling for the discarded weapons. Adrenaline and knowledge that the tide was turning put Bolan in kill-or-be-killed mode. The Executioner buried a fist deep in Rafiz's stomach, then hammered a left hook off the Iranian's jaw. The Iranian took another tumble to the ground.

Bolan turned his sights on Nassir who was less

than three feet from the weapons and was scrabbling hard, kicking up dust and hay like a wild animal about to break out of a cage. Knowing he'd never reach the Iranian in time, Bolan seized the only option available. Legs pumping, the soldier dashed for the pitchfork leaning against the stall.

Nassir snarled something in Farsi, his hands raking in the Desert Eagle.

The Executioner hauled the pitchfork out of the earth, raised it, arm back. Nassir was hitting his knees when Bolan let the pitchfork fly. He heard a wet thud, a scream of pain, then caught sight of the tines that had speared through the back of Nassir. The middle tine had sunk through the spine, severing his spinal cord. Nassir's scream was cut short as nerve circuitry blacked out. It looked as if the Iranian, utterly still with his legs out and his head straining back at a gruesome angle, was impaled to the earth.

A done deal with Nassir, Bolan turned his full attention on Rafiz.

The Iranian rose, then shuffled forward, his face a veil of blood, his eyes bulged by hate and pain. The roundhouse kick craned for Bolan's head, but there was very little behind it. The Executioner ducked the kick, then turned it up a notch. Punishing blows to the Iranian's gut and ribs, followed by lefts and rights that snapped his head side to side as if it was attached to his shoulders by a spring. Bolan pulled back on the blows just enough to keep the terrorist standing and aware of the beating. One more shot, a backhand hammer-fist, and Rafiz had all he could take. The Iranian's legs folded and he pitched to the ground. A groan escaped his lips, but Bolan knew Rafiz was still in the picture.

The Executioner retrieved his weapons, holstered them, then went and grabbed a bucket, scooped out a pail full of slimy water from the trough. A few long strides back to Rafiz, and he doused the man full in the face. The slop revived the Iranian.

Rafiz sputtered, gagging on filth and blood. "All right…all right…enough…"

Bolan sensed he was finally getting somewhere.

"Whatever I tell you…it won't be enough. I know very little."

"I'll be the judge of that. The American who got on your flight in Paris. He was traveling under an assumed identity with a forged passport.

"Yes."

Bolan sucked in a deep breath, teeth clenched to stave off the pain in his side. At least he could breathe without doubling over, meaning there were no cracked ribs from the guy's kick. "You're a first-hand witness. The American?"

A bitter chuckle. "We suspected American FBI or Justice Department agents were on board. It was stupid of us to talk in English."

"Who was he?"

"I have no name."

The Executioner took the Beretta and aimed it at the Iranian's crotch. The expression of fear told Bolan he'd touched a nerve.

"It's true, listen to me."

"But he's American?"

"Yes."

"What is he? CIA?"

"When the shah was in power, they were hired. They trained many of us in interrogation techniques."

"You mean torture."

"One man's torture, well, it's like one man's freedom fighter is another man's terrorist."

"I've heard that. My question."

Rafiz struggled up onto an elbow and closed his legs. Bolan adjusted his aim, compensating by dropping the Beretta's muzzle toward a knee.

"Listen to me. These men were hired by the shah, paid a lot of money to train us. Everything from hand-to-hand combat to small and heavy arms, right before the war with Iraq. We were ordered by the shah himself to treat them as if they were the Prophet, infidels or not. They were said to be the best soldiers money could buy. They sold themselves to whoever had the most money, so I heard. At that time, the shah's oil money made them rich. The shah treated them as if they were Allah. It made some of us sick. They had contacts and connections, I understand, everything from the KGB to the CIA, playing both sides. They brought in weapons, lots of weapons, even nerve gas to be used on the Iraqis."

"For someone who doesn't know much…"

"You hear the talk sometimes, in bars, between

soldiers in the field. At one point SAVAK even tried to pin down the identities of these men. But if too many questions were asked, any loose tongues in SAVAK just vanished. Who knows what to believe? I heard these men are like ghosts, dead men with no identity, no past. I heard they are formerly of your Special Forces. They have been around for a long, long time, if you believe the rumors. They have taken money from every- and anyone who would pay them. African dictators, Colombian drug cartels, trained Arab freedom fighters from Syria to Somalia.''

"And the shah hired them."

"I believe I already said that."

"But you have no names."

"One of them is called the colonel. The rest is only rumor."

"I'm listening."

"I heard they were listed as killed in action in your Vietnam War."

If he hadn't had Rafiz right where he wanted him, at the threshold of death, Bolan wouldn't have believed the man.

"It should be easy enough to verify," Rafiz said.

Maybe, maybe not, Bolan knew. Stony Man Farm would run with whatever he got out of Rafiz. Right then, the soldier was looking for direction.

"My next questions should be obvious."

Rafiz chuckled, wiped blood off his face with the back of his hand. "Two months ago, I was contacted by a man in Tehran, he may or may not have been

CIA. I was given a sum of money and instructions. The war against the Great Satan was about to be launched, I was told. Myself and Nassir were given the necessary paperwork to get to Lebanon and from there...I was only fed intelligence on a need-to-know basis."

"And you were told the colonel would fill you in?"

"Yes. I was given an address to contact once I landed in America."

"Let's have it."

Bolan mentally filed away the address in Fairfax, Virginia.

"I was told I would receive further instructions there."

"What else?"

"What else? I have given you everything I know. Kill me if you want. It will do you no good, it won't stop the colonel."

3

Baptized in honor and forged in blood, in a distant country forgotten by most Americans. Respecting these two ideals had kept the twelve of them alive as a unit and marching toward something that had its strange genesis in what now seemed a hundred lifetimes ago.

And the first rule of any elite fighting unit engaged with the enemy was to overcome the few resources and long odds with good old-fashioned guts and imagination. The second rule, forever the soldier's lurking ghost, was pretty much beyond control.

Murphy's Law.

Right then Colonel Ian Becker could feel the ill winds blowing toward them, and he had all the Murphy he could stomach. He searched the big warehouse and felt alive with anger and promise. The D.C. "war-house," he thought, was another timely gift to the operation from their man who had engineered the resurrection of twelve Special Forces warriors, launching what Becker now thought of as Phantom Alpha Six.

His soldiers from the premeditated failure of the

Operation CongBuster days, plus twenty-five Islamic terrorists were now stretched out on cots in the building. Black-clad forms with shoulder-holstered Colt .45s slept beyond the now-emptied crates which bore the U.S. Customs seal, his on-site force stretched out near the four white oversize vans with U.S. Government logos and plates and the three UPS trucks. A few snores, several bodies twitching in restless sleep, all of them, he was sure, dreaming, maybe even seeing their own fears living out in the grip of personal nightmares. An hour ago a mild sedative had helped Becker's force hit the rack. He understood all too well their anxiety, the prebattle jitters. He didn't need tired troops on his hands the next day, edged out and lacking concentration from little or no sleep. After this night there would be no time for sleep.

Coffee, cigarettes, a last square meal and of course, adrenaline, raw anger and determination would clear any cobwebs beginning at 0900 sharp.

While most of them slept, two of Becker's elite monitored the surveillance cameras in another corner of the warehouse. Minicams on top of the building covered the perimeter on all points of the compass. Security was tight, the grounds monitored around the clock. They had lived in the warehouse for a month, ironing out last-minute details, going over every man's moves in endless briefs, positions, timetables, everything that was expected of each and every soldier. From *A* to *Z* he had covered the plan, factoring in what he hoped were all the what-ifs.

Becker took a reality check.

It was one thing, he knew, to train their Islamic contingent on a dusty corner of Tunisia or take down mock targets in the blistering sands of Syria. It would prove something else altogether to actually do it when the bullets started flying, the bombs started going off, and the whole damn city was going up in flames. And that full-scale evacuation, with the screaming hordes trampling each other to get out while the natives most likely went wild with looting, maybe even the whole country thinking the end of the world was in sight.

Becker smiled to himself about the beauty of it all, the sheer genius and enormity of it.

The three delivery trucks sat in the middle of the warehouse floor, and Becker gave them an approving eye. The smell of fresh paint still hung in the air, but to him it smelled sweet. The phoenix was rising from the ashes.

Becker heard to the voice of his second-in-command growling into the cellular phone with its secured line.

"All present and accounted for? No problems? Outstanding. Get some sleep. You'll be contacted at 1200 hours." Gruff, to the point. As Edward Vinyard repeated the process, touching base with all the designated leaders of their safe houses, Becker couldn't believe for a moment that their day of resurrection was one rising sun away.

Six years in the planning, six months to get men, material and ordnance shipped in. Everything had been laid out to the letter, although not all of them knew the full score. For the Islamic terrorists it was enough that the safe houses were secure, they were in America, legitimized with the necessary paperwork and ready to act out their most murderous fantasies against the Great Satan. With troops in place, two dry runs over, it was up to Becker and company to move them out and get it started. Timing would, of course, prove critical, as it always did in any military operation. Shock force and daring in the face of impossible odds were the order of the day. In just over twelve hours, exactly one hundred men and a few women would thrust the most important city on the planet to the edge of annihilation.

But there were problems at the eleventh hour. Murphy's law.

First the snatch of two ex-SAVAK agents on his payroll at Reagan National airport. Then some trouble during the delivery of the package, something about unwanted eyes having to be made blind. They couldn't go into details on the phone, even though it was a secure line. Finally he was told by Artillon not to worry, everything was under control. All things considered, Becker wasn't worried. Only a few knew the most about the operation, first of all. And those who did were kept close to home. Either way, it was too late to abort the operation. But he knew no one would bail, right down to the unworthiest Islamic fanatic. Their dream to vent their hate and rage on the United States had been made possible by Becker, with, of course, a little help from his friends in the CIA. All systems go.

He stood near the wall looking at the war map of Washington D.C. and its surrounding suburbs. The soft glow of the light from the lamp on the metal desk cast shadows over Becker's lean figure. Dressed in black from turtleneck to combat boots, he was just under six feet tall, tipping the scales at 170 pounds, soaking wet. He didn't look like much in a world where muscle and size seemed to count for heart. Or at least in a country that praised size over substance, style over character, he brooded. How the face of the America he once loved and believed in had changed, and for the worst, he reflected.

Perhaps, though, it had all changed in his mind from the moment he had killed his first VC, up close and personal; when his dreams had died and the boy became a man. He couldn't quite pin down what had changed after taking the life of a man who meant to kill him, but something had gotten in his blood, made it burn and fill his heart with an insatiable hunger for more. Since then there had been plenty of killing, from Southeast Asia to Russia, from Syria to Tunisia, to hiring himself and his men out to the Colombian drug cartels.

A hundred lifetimes, no doubt, but a man can have no life at all if he didn't forge himself in the image of his own will. If nothing else, Becker believed in the destiny of the warrior who stayed true to himself and who kept the world at a comfortable distance.

Time and distance had finally bridged themselves. Thirty-some years was a long time to wait, to stay dead and forgotten. But the wait, he believed, had been worth it.

It had all made sense, especially after he was "killed in action" so long ago. From his grave he had watched the country he had once loved and fought for go soft.

What Americans had become sickened him. All that mattered to them was their money, their jobs and maintaining the status quo. He had no use for people who cared only about the illusion of living well, taking all, giving back little or nothing, while giving the reigns of power to leaders who were clearly corrupt and immoral. Where were the old days, when ships were made of wood, men of iron? Warriors used to save and feed entire nations. They took care of those who could not take care of or defend themselves.

He caught his reflection in the glass partition of his office. A closely cropped head of gray hair, he had a lean face, lined and weathered from age and enduring the harshest elements Mother Nature could hurl at a man. His dark eyes stared back at him, full of fire and determination. He was tempted to think he was looking at a ghost or a shadow of his former self. He quickly looked away as Vinyard said, "Colonel, if you could give me a moment, sir."

It was still colonel, and Vinyard was still his sergeant. He looked at the big man sitting beside the desk. Vinyard's broad face with its high cheekbones was framed by shoulder-length black hair and a goatee. Becker stared into the Sergeant's dark eyes, and for a moment they were brothers in blood again. A hundred lifetimes of memories could have passed between their gazes.

A muffled shriek interrupted the silence. Both men ignored it.

"I'll save you the trouble of what-iffing me, Sergeant." Becker moved behind his desk and opened a drawer. He pulled out a bottle of Wild Turkey. "First, let's have a drink for old-time's sake."

Vinyard rose to his full six foot six inches, went to a cabinet filled with glasses, his muscles rippling like corded steel beneath his sweatshirt. Becker fired up a cigarette, drawing deeply while the sergeant uncapped the bottle and poured two drinks.

"A toast. Here's to wooden ships and iron men," Becker said, lifting his glass. They clinked glasses, then killed their drinks. Vinyard refilled their glasses. "And to the best damn Special Forces warriors to ever rise from the grave."

"And on the eighth day God created the twelve of us." Becker paused, sipped his drink, and studied the scowl on Vinyard's face. "Okay, let's have it. You're worried about the snatch at the airport, that loose tongues are right now sounding off and you fear a platoon of Delta Force and SEALs are going to come crashing through the roof any second."

"We don't have a line on those two. We have to assume the Feds have them."

"They know nothing of real importance."

"As far as we know."

"But Biltman is in the clear?"

"He walked right out of the terminal. Cool as the fucking breeze. If he was tailed, he would know it. He's got the radar for that kind of action."

Becker smoked and smiled. "I wouldn't have expected anything different. Daniel Biltman is more of a ghost than any of us. The man has more identities than a Mob informant in the Witness Protection Program. He has seen more plastic surgery than a fleet of Hollywood starlets."

"Indeed. Here's the situation report. The package was delivered. Some unfriendlies saw our people climbing out of the water but were made believers of the cause."

"I gathered as much."

"All of our people are in place, tucked in."

"Chomping at the bit."

"They're Islamic fanatics."

"We made the right choice. The ones carrying, their special deliveries tomorrow will go the distance, for in Allah they trust. They'll die if they have to, as long as they take out as many of us infidels as possible."

Vinyard shook a cigarette out of the pack and fired up. As he was looking at the war map, his gaze narrowed. "I'm not worried about them proving their mettle, sir."

"Yes, Sergeant. Sixteen separate targets. It's all in the timing, the little sideshows leading to the big event. Give or take, at worst five minutes and all sixteen targets should go down as planned.''

"It's the site for command central I still have a problem with, sir.''

Becker glanced over his shoulder at the red circle drawn over the site in question, between Independence and Constitution Avenues. "It's of no strategic or military importance. I thought we were clear on that?''

"But it's easy to take down and hold.''

"It will be easier pickings than our late KGB buddies who delivered our ADMs and the other package.''

"We've pissed off a lot of bad people, sir.''

"We're going to piss off a few more tomorrow, Sergeant. This one's for us. No more jerking off some Cali flunkies, training Islamic terrorists, shuttling weapons and dope all over the world. I hope you're not just in this for the money, soldier.''

"If I was in this for the money, Colonel, I would have packed up my toys and headed home a long time ago, sir.''

"You have no home, Sergeant. None of us do.''

"No shit.''

"We had no families when we signed on and shipped out. That's why we were chosen.''

"We stood alone, for damn sure.''

"And we still do. We were born out of fear, over fifty years ago. You realize that? The Special Forces were created when this country was neither at war or peace. Korea was up-and-coming, the Russians were going nuclear. Think about it. Born out of fear.

The country needed elite specialists who could do the impossible. We've done the impossible for over thirty years. Well, tomorrow we will be up against the most impossible odds. But when this over, and we've had another round of plastic surgery, we can sit on a beach in the South Pacific somewhere and trade war stories knowing full well we've left our mark on history, that we arrived as warriors. That we beat the impossible odds and shoved it down their throats.''

Vinyard looked as if he wanted to say something but paused as they heard the creak of rusty hinges and saw the iron door open. From a dim ray of light shining in the room from across the hall, a skeletal figure emerged. Becker looked at the black tool kit in the man's left hand, the meat cleaver hanging by his side in the other hand, blood dripping off the blade. The Butcher's white apron was slick with blood. The ex-CIA paramilitary operative he knew as Sampson was a freak show study. A bald head, eyes a gun metal gray, set back in a gaunt face, Sampson's skin was the color of smoke. Becker was reminded of a walking cadaver when he looked at the man.

But Sampson was the man who had made their resurrection possible, and Becker had to acknowledge the Butcher's impressive role.

Becker watched the Butcher walk into the office. Sampson whistled softly, shuddered, grinned. ''That was exhausting.''

The colonel could believe it. He'd seen the Butcher's work up close long ago, in the genesis, as he performed surgery without benefit of anesthesia on Vietcong and innocent peasants. Sampson could use a meat cleaver, among other sharp instruments, like a master magician waved a wand and produced a rabbit out of a hat. Sometimes he worked head to toe, sometimes bottom to top. Whichever way he went Becker could be sure he really didn't want to see what was left behind in the other room.

"Like I always say," Sampson chuckled, "they see no evil, hear no evil and speak no evil. Especially when they can't see, hear or speak. God, I'm good." He walked to the desk. There, he dumped the meat cleaver on the desktop with a loud clatter that jolted and angered Becker. Sampson went and got a glass from the cabinet. If Becker hadn't respected the man's methods for extracting information, he would have erupted in rage. Sampson poured himself a drink.

"Help yourself," Becker said.

"Thanks," he said as he helped himself to a cigarette, too.

"Well?" Becker growled.

Sampson smiled. "Our friend, Mr. Smith, has been liberated from the bondage of earthly flesh. Now I know why I hated working for the CIA so much. You can't trust those bastards. This guy has been on my payroll for years, helping me get you contacts. The whole time he's been playing both ends against the middle."

"Hey, tell me something I don't know."

"I am. This asshole had us under surveillance in Syria. You can thank me again for breaking into his room in Damascus and finding the evidence he had mounted against us and putting the torch to it. So I invited the guy here to D.C. to handle the situation." Sampson chuckled.

"Who else knows about us?"

"No one. He was hoping for one last cash payment from me, meantime he's stalling his own people. He was going to take the money then sink us."

"He told no one in the Company? Didn't even tell his wife, his mistress, whatever?"

"Believe me, he was in no condition to lie."

Becker felt a sense of relief. "Sergeant, make sure this place is mined before we pull out."

"Scorched earth, Colonel. I like your style."

Becker heard but wasn't listening to the ghoul. In his mind he heard the jets screaming over the jungle that day, but they were strafing for a position Phantom Alpha Six no longer occupied. He took a can of lighter fluid from his desk drawer, flipped the nozzle and sprayed the war map with the flammable liquid.

He smelled the napalm, cloying out of the dark caverns of his memory. He took the Zippo, flicked open the lid and rolled the wheel. Flame leapt to life and he put the flame to the edge of the war map. Within seconds fire was racing.

"Scorched earth," he muttered, as he threw the burning map into the trash can.

He breathed in the fumes of burning lighter fluid, and laughed.

4

Bolan felt angry. He had no direction beyond his next hard call. There were too many unanswered questions, the jagged pieces of an ominous puzzle falling all over the place. An enemy with no name, no face. Maybe, all things considered, it was simply flying down Interstate 66 alone in his Crown Victoria rental in the dead of night, replaying the brutal and often bizarre Q and A again and again through his head.

The Executioner kept thinking of ghosts, faceless soldiers at large, former Special Forces men if he believed Rafiz, using their martial skills to arm and train enemies of freedom. And what was the Hour of the Great Cleansing Fire?

Were these Green Berets, gone down in history as killed or missing in action? Was it an elaborate cover-up to keep an entire unit dead and forgotten, or simply missing? Why? KIA or MIA, what was the difference? Gone was gone, dead was dead. Why did he keep thinking of dead soldiers?

Something Rafiz had alluded to jabbed like a needle into his memory of a distant time and place. Ghosts, men with no past, no identity. Special

Forces, like himself, able to do the impossible, under the most dire circumstances.

The answers, he believed, had to come in time, either through the cyber-sleuthing at Stony Man Farm or from blood spilled by his own hand. Before leaving the safe house, he had touched base with Hal Brognola. The big Fed was staying in his office at the Justice Department, rerouting the details of Bolan's hard-earned intel to Aaron Kurtzman and the others at the Farm. Brognola was currently working his own sources and contacts inside the FBI and the CIA.

Still, something nagged at Bolan, telling him he should know exactly who the Iranian was talking about. They had been around for a long, long time, Rafiz had told him, selling their services to the highest bidder. It put them on the map somewhere; at some point someone was bound to know who and what they were. Whoever they were, he believed in his gut that, somehow they had mounted and moved a terrorist army into the country. What did they want? What would they attack? What was the motive, if they were former American fighting men? Money? Acting out twisted rage or killing for the sake of killing? Revenge on a country they maybe felt had slighted and abandoned them?

Bolan pulled off to the shoulder of the road and killed the lights. He took the phone and punched in the number to Brognola's office. They needed a break and he hoped Brognola had something he could sink his teeth into. He heard the big Fed's voice, sounding tired and gruff over the secured line.

"I was just reaching for the phone." Brognola said.

"Tell me we've caught a wave."

"Nothing that will take us into shore, but our people may have a nibble. I have to tell you, Striker, we don't have much to run with, no fault of yours, of course. We need something that's going to show up in a military jacket at Fort Bragg. Even if they are Special Forces killed or missing in action—if we believe our boy Rafiz—it's a long shot, Striker, especially if they've wanted to stay dead for all these years. And say they have: Why?"

"The million dollar question. We know the CIA held hands with the shah and a couple of our mystery men are allegedly trained SAVAK agents. Rafiz claimed they had major drug contacts, too. My guess is they've been all over the map, kept themselves dead or missing, changing identities with plastic surgery, knocking off anybody who got too close or thought they knew who they were. We know a few of the more unsavory paramilitary types in the Company were always jumping into the sack with the cartels. So they could have contracted themselves out to both the CIA and the cartels, working both ends for intel and to fatten offshore accounts, maybe. That's just part of their story, if there is one. It's guesswork at this point. These guys have been around, leaving a lot of dirty deeds in their wake.

Someone on the home team at Langley must have a line on these guys."

"We're chipping away at the stone on our end, but it's going to take some time. They didn't keep records on computers back then. So, forget about Kurtzman tapping into their databases at Fort Bragg. I put in a call down there and got a General Winston on the line. Problem is we can't narrow down a time frame. You're talking about a lot of Green Berets, a lot of years of behind-the-lines operations. Well, you were part of the Phoenix program during the war yourself."

"They wouldn't keep records of assassinations and covert ops anyway. Or if they did, they're buried so deep they'd never see human eyes. What I wanted were a few names, men who were in Special Forces and listed as KIA or MIA. Specifically ones in CTUs."

"That can be arranged, and it has been. Bragg was uncooperative, so I called in a few markers over at the Company, since the CIA ran those counter terror units during the Vietnam War, using both SEALs and Special Forces. I've been able to land you a contact who claims he has a real-life horror story to dump in your lap. Something to do with twelve dead soldiers who have risen from the grave."

"Let's have it," Bolan said, and mentally filed away the name and address in Maryland, and the particulars about his rendezvous. "No details from this contact?"

"He wants to give it to you in person. We don't have much else, so I say run with it. If he's blowing smoke, you'll know. If he's working his own agenda, you'll see it."

"What about my next stop? The address Rafiz gave me"

"The Bear ran it down through the Farm's computers. The house in question was sold through Hastings Realty to Khalif Mustapha, who resold it to Ben Cross, a single guy who works for Mustapha. Mustapha is Syrian, thirty-four years old. He appears legit on the surface. He's been in the country for ten years, put himself through college to earn a couple of business degrees, he's got his green card and his own business. Thriving and on the up-and-up, I might add. He's single and clean as far as legal problems are concerned. He runs a home and personal security company. Tax returns put him at a yearly income in the low six figures. It's called LionHead Security. High-tech stuff catering to your six-figure-and-up crowd out in Potomac and Great Falls. Mustapha also owned two condos and three homes, scattered around the Virginia and Maryland suburbs. You mentioned something earlier about an invading force needing legitimate safe houses in the area."

"You said owned."

"Sold them. Six months ago almost to the day, a one-shot deal. Like magic. This guy does in one day what most real estate salesmen chase after their whole lives. We're having difficulty tracking the real owners; it's a paper trail from hell. For all we know, he may have other properties and other assumed identities.''

''Maybe he just likes to buy and sell real estate as a hobby, something to keep him out of trouble?''

''I hear cynicism.''

''Nothing wrong with your ears. What else?''

Bolan listened as Brognola gave him the address of LionHead Security, which was based in the Tyson's Corner area.

''I'm going to get back to General Winston. He'll play ball next time up or I'll tell him that this happens to be an undetermined threat to national security, and does he want to be the guy to take the flak because he stonewalled the Justice Department at critical mass? I want the good general to fax me all military jackets on any Special Forces soldiers KIA or MIA. Or else.''

Bolan had no doubt Brognola could move mountains when he wanted something badly enough.

''We might have caught another break,'' the big Fed informed Bolan. ''The FBI photographed the American in question at Reagan. They sent me a copy, which Kurtzman is running through Interpol, with Akira using computer imaging on any mug shots we turn up for comparisons.''

''You might just find out the man has a suitcase full of aliases and bad paper. Nothing to pin down his real identity.''

''Maybe. Or maybe behind door number three he might turn up in a military jacket that I'll get from

Fort Bragg. You know our people can do anything with computers, maybe they can match up a few faces.''

''The wonders of high tech.''

''You should try it more often.''

''I guess I'm just a soldier from the old school.''

''Right. Typewriters and rotary phones.''

Bolan chuckled. ''I was thinking more along the lines of up close and personal.''

''I gotcha. Watch your back, Striker. We don't know squat on this one, from numbers to motive. You're on your own. Able Team and Phoenix Force aren't available on this one.''

Not good. Bolan could always use a little help from his Stony Man brothers-in-arms. He offered up a silent prayer for their safe return and successful conclusion to their missions.

The soldier needed to get rolling. It wouldn't be the first time he had walked into the enemy guns with nothing but lethal martial skill and a heart of righteous determination. He didn't fear death, realist enough to know the man with the scythe spares no one, good, bad or indifferent.

But with each campaign he only hoped, if nothing else, that he lived long enough to see the savages fall before he did.

''Striker, you there?''

''Yeah.''

''You sound funny. What's eating you?''

''I was just thinking. Hal, if it turns out our own have somehow sold out…''

Bolan let it trail off and Brognola finished it for him. "I understand. Thank God I know you're not in it for the money or the glory."

"Never was."

"Maybe that's why you're so damn good at what you do. At any rate, good luck and stay in touch."

"Will do," Bolan said, and signed off.

The Executioner flicked on the lights, and drove off. He was still on edge, knew there was only one cure for what ailed him.

Bolan needed to launch his blitz. Sooner or later he would put a face on the enemy, and he would take him down.

THE DREAM of a Palestinian state independent of Israel may not become reality, at least not in his lifetime. Ali al-Fallah Khan accepted that. He was willing to die to make it reality.

Lighting a cigarette, the short, bearded Khan stepped through the sliding glass door. He needed some fresh air and a moment alone. Silence, darkness, cool air.

Outside their safe house, moving beyond the patio, he smoked and indulged his thoughts, visions of dreams about to become reality. Inside, his brothers in the jihad movement were restless, watching porn movies. He couldn't understand their appetite for infidel filth, then reasoned they were in the land of the Great Satan after all, where all manner of obscenity was indulged with all the soulless hunger of an animal. Let them be.

A man's motivation may ultimately come through all forms of sin—only Allah was the true judge—but Khan knew where he stood. He was pure of heart and purpose, and because of his virtue he was about to fulfill his unique destiny. Truly he was blessed.

He deserved to stand alone, rewarded. He had come a long way in his lifetime, he reflected. From a boy, poor as the dirt, his family dying off one by one from starvation or the bullets of Israeli soldiers. Then from an angry young man as a warrior in the PLO, remaining in the refugee wastelands of Gaza and the West Bank, needing the sorrow and anger of his people to feed his righteous anger and drive him back out there to slay the Great Satan. Recruited by brother warriors, he had gone on to kill many Israelis, both soldier and civilian, and he took great pride in the fact that he had shed the blood of his enemies. It didn't matter if they were man, woman or child. He had always been blessed with a divine fate.

Over the years, he had been forced to ground more than once, riding out the hot times when he was being hunted, laying low in Beirut. Always crawling out of the rubble and the shadows to kill his enemies again. He had lived like a lion all of his life, and when he was called to die he would go out with a roar, not a whimper.

He recalled all the fighting he'd witnessed between the religious factions in the streets of Beirut, where it was pretty much brother against brother, father against son. What a terrible waste—Arabs killing Arabs. It was one thing to kill for principle, another thing entirely to be forced to kill other Arabs by the Israelis. Well, the West Bank was nothing but a distant memory now. The boy had grown into a man, clinging to his dream of striking terror into the hearts of his enemies, to shed their blood, to hear them scream and beg for their lives.

It was all about to pay off.

Ali al-Fallah Khan and his brothers in the Holy War were about to bring a taste of Beirut to America. The real beauty of it, though, was that the horror that was about to befall the American devils would be unleashed by their own.

He drew deep on his cigarette and chuckled, feeling strong and alive, the weight of the Colt.45 heavy inside his waistband but making him itch to use it. Yes, he was hungry to see the sun rise, knew he wouldn't be able to sleep. He was seeing visions of explosions, hearing the screams of pain and terror in his head, thinking about all the blood he had spilled in his own life, but it would be nothing compared to what was about to happen in a land he hated so much, a people he so despised.

He started to laugh out loud when something hard and cold came up like a hammer under his jaw. Before he could cry out in alarm he was lifted off his feet, a rag doll tossed about in a storm, with something cold as ice digging into his throat.

He realized there was a knife pressed against his skin. He couldn't scream, couldn't move. A thought formed in his mind, and he knew he would take it with him to Allah.

He realized he was going to die before seeing his dreams come true.

5

The Executioner needed a live one but the smoker wasn't destined to be his songbird.

If there had been any doubt he was led to the right place by Rafiz it was gone. First, Bolan had seen the bulge of the weapon on the smoker. There was also the angry glint of fanaticism in the smoker's eyes that the soldier had seen countless times.

All things weighed and considered, Bolan was still going in blind. He lifted his mark a few inches off the ground, dragging him away from the open patio door into the deeper shadows.

"How many inside?" Bolan growled into his mark's ear.

"For you, too many."

Bolan dug the blade a little deeper into the man's throat, drawing a thin trickle of blood. "Wrong answer. One more try. How many?"

"Four."

"Where?"

Bolan could feel the defiance swell in the man's body and knew the fanatic wasn't going to give up anything else.

"Go to hell."

"You first," the warrior said and sliced the gunner's throat from ear to ear, taking out the jugular and vocal cords, shoving the hardman's scream back down his throat in a gurgle of blood.

"Ali?"

Problems.

Bolan was wiping the blade on the back of Ali's pant leg, sheathing the commando dagger and pulling his sound-suppressed Beretta 93-R when a tall shadow emerged from just inside the open door to the basement area. The enemy was no doubt tuned in, hopped up on adrenaline. It stood to reason they would be on high alert, in the country illegally with some agenda of wholesale slaughter.

Bolan went to grim work, even as he realized he may not sack a prisoner. On the fly, the Executioner stroked the Beretta's trigger. A 9 mm hole was punched between the eyes of the shadow, snapping his head back. The shadow tumbled backward, falling hard and loud, a pistol flying from the hardman's hand.

Two down, three to go, if he chose to believe the word of a dead fanatic.

Bolan was through the door, the Beretta leading the way when he tracked a fat bearded man in white underwear and undershirt. Not exactly dressed for combat but the AK-47 in the gunner's fists was up and sweeping around for the big invader.

Bolan ended the man's search with a lightning head shot. The problem was that the gunner had triggered off a dying reflex, spinning around, the

AK-47 spitting out a few rounds. He held his ground for a long moment, then folded at the knees but not before his line of 7.62 mm slugs blasted out the TV screen beside him in a shower of glass and sparks.

To his right, Bolan heard the pounding of footsteps. They were coming down the stairs, two left, he hoped. A noisy hit was the last thing he wanted, but Bolan had to play out the bad cards thrown his way. He needed to wrap this up and bolt. The least he could do there was exterminate one nest of savages.

Bolan flung himself over the couch as two figures hit the bottom of the steps and began filling the room with flaming AK-47 autofire. They were screaming and cursing in Arabic, hosing the room with bullets.

Bolan had one option. He pulled the flash-stun grenade from his windbreaker and yanked the pin. He scuttled for the far end of the couch as stuffing flew over his head and bullets drilled through cushions behind him. He counted off the doomsday numbers, then took a chance as autofire pounded the position he had abandoned. Popping up, Bolan pitched the flash-stun, dropping again as he squeezed his eyes shut and covered his ears. Even still, in the tight confines of the basement the flash and thunder knifed his senses. He rode out the sound and fury, buffeted from the brunt of the force by the couch.

Bolan came up as the two Arabs were reeling all over the place, blinded and senseless. Somehow they held onto their weapons. The strength of madmen, Bolan supposed.

They went back to spraying autofire and Bolan was left with no choice but to end it. A head shot each and he sent them crashing into the wall.

Ears ringing, his nose choked with cordite and raining dust, the soldier looked to a doorway at the end of the hall that ran past the stairs. From his quick surveillance of the house, he knew the door led to the garage. He didn't have time to search the entire house for any intel that would lend him insight into the enemy's agenda. But he wanted something other than five dead fanatics to show for his trouble. He wasn't sure why, a sixth sense perhaps, but he felt something important was behind the door. Swiftly Bolan moved down the hall, watching his rear. He put a foot to the door and sent it flying open. He fumbled his hand along the wall, found a light switch and flicked it up.

And Bolan discovered he had just walked into a small armory. A cursory glance showed a few RPG-7 rocket launchers and five AK-47s leaning against the wall. There were two steamer trunks in one corner and Bolan went and opened them. In one trunk he discovered a mixed assortment of two, maybe three dozen Russian F-1 and RG-42 hand grenades.

The Executioner didn't have to pick up what he found in the other trunk, to know what it was.

Plastic explosive.

"ROUND THEM UP and bail. I want you here twenty minutes ago. Copy that, soldier?"

Becker heard Artillon affirm the order, then signed off. He stood there, not believing what he'd just heard. He felt as if he could snap the cellular phone in two, rage boiling in his gut, fear in his heart. All the work, the planning, the ambition of a lifetime now in jeopardy.

Becker saw Sampson lift himself into a sitting position on the cot. The ghoul had taken a combat nap in his stained apron.

"What?" The Colonel bored an piercing stare into the Butcher.

"Artillon went out to check on some of our people. One of our safe houses was hit. I don't have the particulars, but Fairfax County's finest now has the place swarmed and sealed. Artillon saw five of our Palestinian confederates wheeled out in body bags."

"Who? How?"

Becker showed his teeth in a snarl. "Is Smith still breathing?"

"What? You're joking, right?"

"You hear me laughing, mister?"

"He's nothing but a torso."

Becker's hand trembled as he took a cigarette and torched it with his Zippo. "Did you check for a pulse or just assumed you liberated him?"

"No."

"Do it. I don't think your interrogation went far enough."

The Butcher stood. "How the hell can he talk with no tongue?"

"He has two holes in his head where his ears

were, meaning he can still fucking hear. Meaning he can grunt to simple yes or no questions. If he's still breathing ask him again if anyone knows about us being in the country. Move it!''

The Butcher grumbled but left the office. Becker smoked and told himself to pull it together. He felt Vinyard's presence as the Sergeant filed into the office.

"Sir?"

Becker told Vinyard the situation. "Someone is either onto us or thinks they're onto us," Becker said.

"The others' arrival here, sir. That changes things.''

"I'll have to reroute, that's all. I can't step up the timetable. We had it nailed according to traffic.''

"What do we know about this hit?''

"Zero. If that's what it was. I sent our specialist to see if Smitty's still breathing. Damn it! My gut tells me his SAVAK boys did some singing to the Feds. Fortunately they didn't know enough.''

"But the Palestinians? They were part of our C-link, Colonel.''

"I'm banking they went down with their ship. Praise to Allah and all that crap. So you go in with five less guns, Sergeant. We're still a lock.''

Vinyard looked agitated and reached for the bottle of Wild Turkey. "I don't like it. If the Feds step in—and they will when they find the ordnance in that house—we could be looking at checkpoints, heightened security tomorrow, roadblocks.''

Becker took another drag on his cigarette. "If so much as a wino shows up on camera, Sergeant, I want our people up, armed and ready for anything. Hell, you see a blue-and-white out there, so much as within spitting distance, I want them iced and handed over to Sampson to be sliced and diced."

The Butcher came back and shook his head.

Becker cursed.

"I hope you're not planning on pissing on what I've spent an entire lifetime putting together, Colonel," Sampson said. "I played hell to make and keep you dead all these years. Money, retribution, a statement, each man will get what he wants. We will not fail."

THE EXECUTIONER found the back door to the warehouse unlocked, just as Brognola said he would. It was one of the particulars for this rendezvous Bolan didn't like. A simple walk-in, some give-and-take with two unknowns who were supposedly on the home team. It was dicey all around. Bad past experience with the CIA warned Bolan to keep up his guard, not trust anything at face value.

This wouldn't be the first time Brognola had called in a marker over at Langley. Some company contacts were legitimate, had even aided a particular campaign in the past. Others had proved true to only their own agendas, sometimes putting Bolan unwittingly on the firing line, the soldier left wondering who was who, what was what.

Whatever, the men Bolan would meet now were

specialists, meaning they fell in some murky abyss between a paramilitary operative and a Company assassin. They were the best of the worst the CIA kept on its payroll. Their agenda was subterfuge, sabotage and stone-cold killing. Officially they didn't exist. Unofficially they did the sort of black ops that kept the politicians screaming on Capitol Hill for either total control or dismantling of the CIA. The soldier knew whatever hard intel he could glean on his nameless enemies might come from just such operatives who lived in the Company's dirty trenches. He could only trust his instincts.

Bolan gave the empty lot one last search. Before arriving at the warehouse in Rockville the soldier made a drive-by of LionHead Security in Tyson's Corner. A light had been on in the town house office, but Bolan had resisted the urge to have a conversation with the owner. Khalif Mustapha was next on his shopping list.

Bolan moved into the warehouse and shut the door behind him. The place was empty with no sign of life except for two shadows in the far corner of the building. They were outlined in the soft glow from a single naked bulb hanging above them in the glassed office. Standard side arms in place, Bolan walked across the empty warehouse, checking the catwalks and his surroundings.

"Just the three of us, Belasko," a deep bass voice rumbled from the office.

Closing, Bolan studied the two men, who sat around a metal table in the middle of the office. At the head of the table sat a black man with a shaved skull, dressed in a gray turtleneck and jeans. The other operative sat against the wall. Outfitted in a black sport shirt and pants, his snow-white crew cut gave his pale, sharp features a ghoulish touch. Each had 9 mm Berettas in a shoulder holster.

The black agent gestured toward the metal chair at the opposite end of the table. Bolan held his ground beside the table, glancing at the briefcase on the floor.

"I'm Johnson," the black op said.

"Jackson," the other one told Bolan.

"Okay," Bolan said, slowly taking a seat. "Now tell me what you've got."

"The Apocalypse," Johnson said.

"Armageddon, USA."

Bolan clenched his jaw. "I'm a little busy tonight."

"Relax. Sit."

Bolan didn't budge. Johnson reached down, pulled a thick manila envelope from his briefcase. He dumped it on the table, rested his hand on top of it and said, "Please."

The soldier sat.

"There are twelve of them," Johnson began. "I've got their CIA file in here, your eyes only, complete with my own report, which I hasten to add, comes from some personal experience during long years of tracking them. Your boss carries weight, Belasko. I was ordered to hand this over on pretty much an or-else proposition. My gift to you is complete with photos and background information. They were supposedly killed in Vietnam, then listed as missing in action. Just for starters.''

''A few of these new apostles were Medal of Honor winners,'' Jackson said. ''Heroes. Might even have their names on the Memorial Wall. I don't know, haven't checked lately. I don't care. I just want them put out of business. It's bad for the CIA's image.''

''They've been around for three decades, Belasko, doing all kinds of dirty shit for all kinds of dirty people. It's all in the package.''

''I've got to ask,'' Bolan said. ''What's in it for you?''

''Peace of mind,'' Johnson said.

''We were ordered to wash our hands of this,'' Jackson added.

''Read the package, you'll see these guys are proved talent. They were part of the Phoenix program.''

''I know about the program,'' Bolan said.

''Is that right?''

''I was Special Forces myself,'' Johnson told Bolan. ''CTUs they called them.''

''More commonly known now as PRUs,'' Jackson chimed in to the singsong act. ''Provincial Reconnaissance Units. The Army didn't like anything that sounded too much like special warfare, visions of My Lai maybe, all that. Blood-thirsty barbarians.''

Johnson shrugged. "Didn't want to upset the civilian populace back in the world, I guess."

"PRUs. The Army went politically correct before the rest of the country did."

"Are they here?" Bolan asked, tiring of their routine.

Johnson shrugged. "Hard to say. I'd say yes."

"I'd say you're right. I made a preemptive strike."

Jackson lifted an eyebrow. "Do tell."

Bolan did.

"They're here," Johnson said, nodding.

Bolan had a lot of questions, but if what he needed was in the file he could take it to Brognola and have Stony Man Farm dissect it. The Executioner felt a growing urgency to get out of there. Unless he missed his guess, war was about to be declared on American soil.

Johnson slid the package toward Bolan. "Thanks for stopping by."

Bolan stood and took the package. He turned to leave but Johnson called out, "Hey."

Bolan looked back.

"Good luck and good hunting."

The Executioner watched the black op gather his things to leave. A time bomb was ticking in Bolan's gut. He might hold a few clues to hand Brognola, but something told the Executioner he was about to face something that every American had only up to then feared—a full-blown frontal assault by a terrorist army.

6

"Striker, I'm beginning to think what we've really got is a handful of light and shadow. In short, we've got squat."

"I'm not so sure, Hal."

Bolan had taken the ghost file straight to Brognola's office at the Justice Department. The big Fed was now pacing behind his desk, a human grenade of nerves and agitation. Wooden boards were nailed to the broken office windows behind him, the light burning from a lone lamp on his desk. Dawn was an hour or so away. Bolan figured the rush-hour commute was about to swell the city with its workforce. It would be another normal workday out there, but a day of fear and uncertainty was the order of business for Bolan, Brognola and the Stony Man team. Bolan knew they had serious problems. Worse, they had no clearly defined direction. At the very least they had put a face on the enemy, along with twelve names. It was a start, but Bolan felt like they were hardly in the ballpark.

Brognola looked weary and worried. The big Fed was a juggling act of black coffee, a cigar and a pack of antacid tablets. Bolan figured it would be easier to shave the stripes off a tiger than try to tell Brognola to relax.

As soon as they had pored over the CIA file and the military facts General Winston had sent to Brognola, the big Fed had photocopied the pertinent intel and faxed it on to the Farm.

The phone on Brognola's desk rang. Picking it up, he growled, "Yeah." The dark scowl on Brognola's face told Bolan there was bad news on the other end. "Turn them inside out, upside down. I hear you. I don't care what it looks like, Collins. Dust them for prints. Everything, down to the toilet seats, the vents, a crack in the wall. That's right, all five of them. Call me back when you're finished. Whatever you get I want it on my desk before the sun rises."

Brognola put the phone down hard. "Damn. Those teams I told you I sent out to the properties Mustapha sold after you took down those five hostiles? Empty. Looks like nobody ever lived there. Nothing in all five locales, not even a beer in the fridge. It's like a UFO descended on these places and whisked everything up to the stars."

"I'm not surprised."

"Nor I. Get this. An hour ago, a memo landed on my desk, and right after the Bear did some digging on Hastings Realty. We popped Hastings a week ago, after a joint ongoing DEA and Justice Department investigation. They were laundering money, moving real estate around like chess pieces, while moving cocaine out of their home office in

Arlington. Problem is we've got one American, a con man with a criminal record, and one Lebanese national who ran Hastings Realty and they're not talking anything but deal, a sweetheart deal that gives them full immunity.''

"You might give it consideration.''

"I'm annoyed with myself I missed that piece of our puzzle before now, but that's what I'm considering.''

"With everything on your plate, it's understandable.''

Brognola grumbled something Bolan couldn't understand. The soldier picked up his own cup of coffee and drank deeply sitting in his chair in front of the Fed's desk. "Everything leads to our boy Mustapha again, Hal. Mr. Clean is starting to smell.''

"Well, he's built himself a nice wall.''

"I can go over that wall, or through it.''

Brognola rested his dark stare on Bolan. "You said you think we're in the back seat of something the likes of which this country's never seen. But what? A full-scale terrorist attack on the city? By twelve Special Forces men who were made to disappear more than thirty years ago? Now they rise from the dead and are in the country with maybe a terrorist army in their back pockets, everyone foaming at the mouth to do us, the Great Satan, in? How do I sell that to the President?''

"That wasn't a Mideast peace delegation I neutralized in Virginia. You could start by telling the Man about that. As far as those sudden vacancies,

I'm betting someone was tipped off, maybe put in a call to that safe house. When there was no answer, they became nervous and ordered the rest of the troops to bail to a secondary location. Again Mustapha. More and more I want him for a serious face-to-face.''

Brognola frowned, then sighed. ''I've got a team pulling rank on Fairfax County police as we speak. I'm trying to keep this out of the papers, trying to avoid a general panic, but with the neighbors, the cops out there scratching their heads...Anyway the word from my special agent-in-charge on-site is that what you found was, indeed, plastique. No ID on the five hostiles, not a shred of anything in the house to tell us who they were. What a surprise, huh? I'm told the plastic explosive weighed in at close to a hundred pounds. Primers, detonator cords, the whole package ready for special delivery. But what the hell are they after? Are we looking at another Oklahoma City, upgraded to a new level of destruction? If so, what are they going to blow up?''

Bolan took a drink of his coffee before responding. ''Anything. Everything. With a city this size, you're looking at any hundred possible targets. Where's the President?''

''In town.''

''Do you know his agenda?''

''No. But I'll be talking to him ASAP. The problem is, we don't have anything concrete to report, Striker.''

''We know who they are.''

"Right. Ghosts. Dead soldiers." Brognola clenched his jaw. "Do you think this is about the President?"

"I'm in the dark as much as you are, Hal. But I'd cover all bases. The Man needs to be told something. And he needs to know that whatever happens you and you alone are in charge. Not the Pentagon or any dozen or so alphabet soup agencies."

Brognola peered at Bolan. "You expect a major disaster, a war, a siege, don't you?"

"That's what my gut is telling me. It's just a question of when and where."

Brognola began to pace with his coffee cup in hand. "Dead men. Made to vanish over thirty years ago. Had their hands in drugs, guns, terrorist training, if you believe what we've got."

"For Johnson and Jackson to hand over what the CIA has put together on these guys, someone in the Company is either nervous or has grown a guilty conscience."

"Okay," Brognola said, as he sat in his chair. "Let's look at that for a minute. We've gone over Fort Bragg's facts and Johnson and Jackson's report. Nothing revealing out of Bragg, other than these guys were born in the U.S.A. and grew to be professional soldiers. Okay. Johnson was Special Forces, part of the CTUs at the time these twelve were supposedly blown to kingdom come. The CIA knew about these guys, maybe for years, only they were chasing the wind."

"Or they gave the appearance of chasing the

wind," Bolan suggested. "I was told they're proved talent. That's enough for me to buy they've been able to stay buried and forgotten up to now. From what we've learned none of it is beyond possibility. These twelve, Phantom Alpha Six, were on a search-and-destroy along the Cambodian border. They called in an air strike."

"But, called in the wrong coordinates. They were napalmed not just once, but twice. I can buy one SNAFU, but two in one day, same time, same place. That's Murphy's Law working overtime. What little we gleaned from the spook package tells us the bombing team left a smoking crater in the jungle the size of five city blocks. They had to make sure the tunnel rats—VC dug in below the earth—were neutralized. And the military did an investigation."

"Or appeared to do so," Bolan said.

"No matter how much napalm was dropped, a few skeletons should have turned up, but didn't. So you bypass the problem of bodies and dental records, hell, it looks like they didn't even find a dog tag. We can't even nail down where they operated out of back then, not even a forward operating base. If there were any reports, debriefs, it was like somebody took a magic wand and made it all disappear into a puff of smoke."

"The CIA believed it was on a power trip during that war. They did pretty much whatever they wanted to do, good, bad or indifferent. We know the type."

"But why the cover-up?"

"If I can find the answer to that we might know why they're here and what they've got planned."

Brognola frowned. "I can tell the President to beef up security, we've got a potential terrorist threat in the city. I can have security tightened in and around the Capitol, all federal buildings, maybe. It's stretching resources, but without a solid lead as to the whereabouts of the others...This is comparable to what cops face when they've got a serial killer. The only time they catch a break is when the killer strikes again and makes a mistake."

"They've already made a mistake. They brought their two SAVAK cronies on board, my guess to maybe shore up one hit team. But I took care of Rafiz and Nassir in the barn."

"Hey, no criticism there, Striker, but my people were a little shaken by your interrogation methods."

"It's a tough life."

"That's what I told them. Anyway. Let's go over this again. Twelve soldiers, young guys, all volunteers. Common denominator? Single guys, little if any family back home. What family they had died within two to three years of their MIA status."

"They were chosen. Men who wouldn't be missed."

"Again, chosen for what? By whom?"

"What do we know about Colonel Ian Becker?"

Brognola grunted. "CIA. Black ops. Mr. Enigma, Agent Smoke and Mirrors. Probably worked both sides, opium, gunrunning. You've seen the type. Lining his pockets, had his own little hit team out there burning up the bush, either killing or making deals with the VC.''

''That's ancient history. We need to concentrate on tracking them down.''

Brognola snapped up the phone. ''Let me see if Kurtzman's come up with something.''

Bolan waited while the big Fed punched in the numbers, going through a series of cutouts before reaching Stony Man Farm. The Executioner waited until he heard Aaron Kurtzman's voice come over the speaker phone.

''Bear?'' Brognola said, using Kurtzman's nickname. ''We need some good news.''

Bolan listened as Kurtzman said, ''I've got news, but it isn't good. I'm going to lay it all out and I think we can come up with two and two. Here it is. There was a Web site address in your spook package. Turns out it was the database for LandSat. As you may know, LandSat searches for oil and other minerals around the world. It also monitors Russian crops, namely wheat, the idea being we need to know if the Russians are starving or lying about their food supplies. That translates into are they looking for a handout from their Western comrades? This is where it gets ugly. LandSat picked up something in a remote region of Kazakhstan.'' Kurtzman paused, then said, ''I'm looking at a hot zone, gentlemen. There was a nuclear explosion in this region recently. The blast radius was just over one mile.''

Bolan felt his blood race as he stared into Brognola's eyes.

"They passed this onto NORAD, supposedly," Kurtzman went on, "but there was nothing in the NORAD databases other than what they received through the satellite imagery."

"Meaning they wanted to keep it quiet," Brognola said.

"Or they don't have enough intel," Kurtzman replied, "or the Russians are covering it up in the name of glasnost. The obvious question is why would your specialists pass this on? Further, I did some digging into the databases at the U.S. Embassy in Moscow. The CIA had a line on four ex-KGB agents who supposedly had access to what could have caused this blast. These ex-KGB were renegades, rumored to have worked with the Russian Mafia, deemed mentally unstable by their own. All right, we already know the Russians more than likely have developed their own version of our Special Forces nuclear backpack."

"And it was up for sale," Bolan said.

"It would appear so, Striker. Question is, who bought it? From what I tapped into, those former KGB agents are missing. The buyers, I'm thinking, never meant to play a straight deal with their KGB pals."

"Convenient," Brognola groused.

"Too convenient. So, we have to presume whoever bought the Russian version of the Special Forces Atomic Demolition Munition was tying up loose ends. Bang, bang, have a nice day, thanks for your help.'' With dead air on Kurtzman's end, Bolan could feel Brognola's tension rise a few notches.

''Are we all on the same page here?'' Brognola finally asked, grimly. ''Are you telling me, Bear, that maybe our twelve dead soldiers ripped off the Russians after they tested a Soviet ADM in Kazakhstan, then smuggled it out of the country?''

''If they did they're playing true to form. I've done the homework. I tapped into the DEA databases. Our guy who slipped through the net at Reagan National Airport has been identified as Daniel Biltman, United States Special Forces. He was one of the chosen. Since we were talking about mercenaries selling their services to the highest bidder, and since the drug angle was mentioned in this spook package, I did some serious digging. Akira and I put our computers together and have done some interesting things here with computer imaging. I've got Interpol, DEA, FBI photos and files, and we've been matching up the players in question, their faces with each alias. I've got aliases from Peter Paul to Paul John to Paul Peters to John Solomon.''

''Cute,'' Brognola growled. ''Keeping in character with their resurrection image.''

''I don't know what Striker plans to do, but I'm sure he's anxious to get moving. Maybe on this Mustapha. My read on Khalif Mustapha is that he's somehow involved with our twelve new disciples. At any rate, I'm going through phone records, his financial records, whatever I can sink my teeth into to get Striker on track.''

"Send the package, Bear," Brognola said, then fell silent.

The Executioner found the big Fed staring at him, felt Brognola's tension hitting him like a sudden heat wave.

"Striker, we have got definite problems."

7

The first target for Phantom Alpha Six was the republican senator from Maryland.

Christopher Walker was ex-Corps, a decorated Vietnam vet, in fact, with a Purple Heart and a Medal of Honor. He had two sons, ages twelve and thirteen, and was married to the same woman for twenty years. No skeletons in his closet, a clean bill of moral health. He had followed up two tours of duty by putting himself through law school on the G.I. Bill, went on to build his own successful law firm before landing a career as a Senator that now had him in his third term. He was a favorite among the people, out there pitching for the middle class, big on jobs and education, but tough on crime, especially gun control. Contributed sizable donations to a number of charities and hospitals, he was a likable guy who went out there and rubbed shoulders with the voters. All in all not much ammunition for his political opponents to fire off during re-election campaigns.

Phantom Alpha Six could be in for a fight. No easy pickings, perhaps, but Max Kelly knew they had done their homework, enough so that they could get in, take down and hold the fort.

Until the beginning of the end was officially underway.

Kelly ran the numbers through his mind again. Okay, two kids, the wife, the live-in housekeeper, an old widow, Cecilia, no sweat. Then, of course, there was the driver, an armed one-man security force, another former Marine, a problem that would have to be neutralized outside the gate.

Through binoculars Kelly watched the driver standing by the Lincoln Towncar at the end of the circular driveway, waiting on the boss. A week of recon and study had shown that the senator stuck to the same daily routine. Off to work at eight sharp, after seeing the kids to the bus stop. The wrought-iron front gates were always open to allow quick exit at that hour of departure. There was very little by way of security, other than a few alarms, if the intel was on the money. But this was Potomac, Maryland, after all, the suburban fortress of the rich, no one ever looking to purchase serious real estate out here unless they had seven figures to burn.

All things considered, it was always easiest when they were creatures of habit.

Kelly told his driver, Scott, "Roll it in easy." Kelly's well-defined muscles rippled beneath his white coveralls as he turned in his passenger seat and glanced into the back of the van. The other two Syrian confederates, Fasrah and Jamal, were gripping the large black tool bags, their dark eyes blazing with angry intent and hunger to get on with it. "By the numbers, gentlemen, just as I laid it out. No fuckups, and obey my orders at all times. Am I clear?" Shaky nods didn't convince Kelly they were on the same page. "I said, am I clear?"

They responded with a little more enthusiasm when Kelly put the right amount of steel in his eyes and voice.

Kelly faced forward as Scott eased the white van—which bore the painted logo of Jeffrey Plumbing—past the open gates. Right away, Kelly saw the security guard snap to attention. The adrenaline started to burn in Kelly's veins, as he spotted the bulge of the pistol beneath the guy's jacket. Kelly ran his hand over his short black hair, caught sight of the grim determination in his own blue eyes as he glanced into the sideview mirror. All clear. Nobody within view on the street in either directions. It had to be done quickly, with little fanfare.

For a moment, Kelly looked at the massive brick and stone dwelling, a walled estate surrounded by lots of shrubbery and trees, with a marble-columned front facade. A little shopping two weeks earlier as a potential buyer for a home out here, and Kelly had nailed the layout of the target site. There was a lot of territory for four men to cover, upstairs and down, but he knew the family was assembled in the living room, if they played true to habit. The plan was laid out; all they had to do was execute.

It was game time.

The van stopped and Kelly disembarked, sporting

his best disarming smile. The security guard was
headed his way, suspicious.

"Can I help you?"

"Yes, sir," Kelly said, reciting the address to the
security man. "Someone called in, yesterday; Cecilia the housekeeper it was. Something about the
shower upstairs not working and a backed-up toilet.
Sounds like maybe we need to run a snake through
the works, Chief."

The Syrians were out of the van, lugging the
black kits. The security guard knew something
wasn't right, instinct taking over, but Kelly had anticipated as much from a Marine.

"Nobody called any plumbers. What the—"

The sound-suppressed Beretta 92-F came out of a
deep pocket in Kelly's coveralls to blast the ex-
Marine's anger back into his throat. A tap of the
trigger and Kelly drilled a 9 mm round into the
man's open mouth, the slug coring on, punching out
the back of his skull in a spray of scarlet muck.

Kelly was past the security man, already bound-
ing up the steps, the front doors open as they always
were at that time of the morning. Beyond he heard
the senator's voice calling, "John! What's going on
out there?"

Kelly saw Fasrah scoop up the body, struggling
with the bulky weight in a fireman's carry. Jamal
and Scott were on his heels, digging the hardware
out of their black bags.

A head of closely cropped gray hair appeared in

the doorway. Kelly glimpsed the handsome, square-jawed face full with fear, then sudden anger.

"Julie, call the police!"

The senator almost had the doors slammed in Kelly's face, but Kelly bulldozed his way past the heavy oak doors, driving Walker down the foyer, skidding on his butt. A flurry of activity in the living room, the shouts of alarm, and Kelly knew they had to move quickly. They may have had big money, prestige and status, all the trappings of the good life, but Kelly clearly saw these people if threatened, were ready to fight dirty.

Not good.

"The phones!" Kelly roared as the Syrians charged into the foyer.

Walker nearly proved Kelly's worst fear about the takedown. He heard the growl of rage and saw the raw determination in the ex-Marine's eyes a heartbeat before the fist hammered him in the jaw. As the lights nearly blinked out in Kelly's eyes, he heard Walker roar, "You bastards!"

The ex-Marine was cranked up, the male lion protecting his den from the jackals. Somehow Kelly kept himself from tumbling to the foyer, knew he was too far into it to lose it now. Through the mist in his eyes he saw Jamal had hauled the Heckler & Koch MP-5 submachine gun from the black bag. Shaking the cobwebs from his head, Kelly then discovered Walker was hell-bent on fighting back some more.

Fasrah dumped his dead weight, had his own subgun out before charging into the living room, screaming, "Don't move! Or I'll shoot. On your knees, all of you! Do it, damn you, do it now!"

Jamal went for the phone by the couch, ripping the cord out of the wall. Kelly was forced to focus all attention on Walker as the senator came at him like an enraged bull. He ducked the looping round-house kick and decided he'd had enough. With all his strength, he buried a fist deep into the senator's stomach, then clipped him over the ear with the barrel of his Beretta. The senator dropped to his knees.

"Grab the kids!" Kelly ordered. "Scotty, check the house!"

Wife, kids and housekeeper were all present and accounted for, but Kelly needed to check the place, just the same. Jamal and Fasrah snatched both sons and shoved the muzzles of their weapons under their chins. The wife, a pretty brunette, shapely in all the right places, Kelly thought, was screaming, "Don't shoot them, for the love of God, don't!"

"Shut up!" Kelly roared. Worried about all the racket they had made coming in, he looked to the doors. At least one of his Syrian teammates had had the presence of mind to shut the doors on the way in. "Nobody's going to get shot if you do exactly as you're told!"

"I swear, you harm my family, I'll kill you with my bare hands."

Kelly stared into the senator's eyes, which were filled with anger and hate. Walker stood and let the blood trickling from the gash in the side of his head run down his face. Kelly believed the former war hero would do his damnedest to honor that threat. Kelly stepped back, the Beretta low by his side.

"What do you want? Money? You want money?"

"No," Kelly said. "This isn't about money, sir."

Walker narrowed his gaze, confused. "'Sir?'"

"Yes, sir. This is about a middle-finger salute. It's about the glory days."

"What the hell are you talking about?"

"I'll explain later, Marine. First, have your lovely wife call the school to explain the boys will be out for a few days with the flu. Then call your office and tell them you had to leave town for a few days. Your sister upstate is sick. The widow housekeeper over there doesn't have anybody for pillow talk. So, if you don't do what I tell you, she'll be the next to go, since she won't be missed. Well, soldier?"

"Do I have a choice?"

"No. I don't even have a choice anymore, but I never did."

Kelly chuckled in the face of the ex-Marine's anger and confusion. All systems were go.

INTELLIGENCE was only as good as the man using it. The problem was the Executioner had a few nibbles, but nothing he could sink his teeth into.

Bolan was about to attempt to change that situation.

He parked the Crown Vic at the doorstep to LionHead Security. The three-story town house complex was the sole property of Khalif Mustapha, with the Syrian keeping two dozen employees on his payroll, according to Kurtzman's digging. However he found too many employees inside. The soldier, needing some time alone with Mustapha, prepared to use both his Justice Department ID and a little muscle, if necessary. He would let Mustapha call the action.

Kurtzman had dug up an interesting tidbit on Mustapha, and Bolan was going to use that piece of intel as a lead-in to shake the tree of LionHead's boss. Gut instinct told Bolan the Syrian was dirty somehow, but he needed more than a hunch.

The soldier's long topcoat covered his standard side arms, but more than a cursory glance would send a shiver of alarm through anyone with something to worry about. Bolan was betting Mustapha was the worrying type.

Glancing at the LionHead logo on the door, Bolan turned the knob. The door buzzed as he went into the office. A young man with a ponytail and gold earring looked up from behind his desk. Bolan had his badge and credentials already out.

"It's your boss in?"

The man looked concerned, his mouth working to find words. "Y-yes...back office. Take...the hall." The man started to call out, but Bolan warned him, "I'll announce myself. How many people are in this office?"

"Six."

"Round them up; all of you grab some air. A long early lunch down the street."

As he moved Bolan caught sight of a shadow down the hall. The Executioner was strolling toward the back as he heard the man with the ponytail gather the workforce. The soldier was forced to eat up a few moments while they trooped downstairs, casting him wary looks. Bolan was then forced to haul out his Justice Department ID. They filed out, but Bolan suddenly felt something was wrong with the setup.

He heard movement from beyond a doorway at the end of the hall. They were hasty movements, like someone in a hurry to get to something. Combat instincts kicking in, Bolan pulled his Beretta 93-R from his shoulder rigging. The Executioner pulled up just beyond the doorway and risked a look inside. He locked eyes with Khalif Mustapha.

The Syrian was digging into a desk drawer. The situation felt more wrong to Bolan with each passing heartbeat.

He quickly discovered why.

If the Syrian was such a legitimate citizen of the United States and an aboveboard businessman, then the Executioner wondered why Mustapha was hauling a .357 Magnum Colt Python from his desk and swinging it toward a man who had announced he was from the Justice Department.

The Executioner sighted down the Beretta.

MARTIKA KOBESLAV was dressed in black for her morning rendezvous. In fact, she was dressed to kill.

The long-legged, blond Czech daubed on a smear of red lipstick, then tucked the lipstick away in her purse, smoothed her short black leather skirt and began the strut to the waiting limo. Her high heels clicked along the concrete of the parking garage, her pulse quickening against the sound of each advancing step with the knowledge of what she was about to do. Giving her silky mane a toss of the head, she looked around, spotted her backup, two dark figures up front in the Chevy van, a third in the back. She would need them for the finishing touches, as planned, but she was the one responsible for getting it started.

The mark was a democratic senator from Virginia who fancied himself a real stallion when it came to the ladies, but who had fallen way short in that department in her eyes. The playboy politician was all ego and vanity, and she was left wondering if there were any real men left in the nation's capital, where it was all about pushing paper and image, crunching numbers and screwing thy neighbor's wife.

It had been easy enough, catching his eye in his favorite Capitol Hill watering hole, warming up to him after he got loose on a few martinis. Going in she had been well versed on his adulterous track record, his eye for shapely unescorted females, but with the need to be discreet, of course. It was all part of the intel package dropped in her lap from her principal. She had done this sort of thing in the past for the Russians when the cold war was still hot and the KGB needed to exploit a few CIA agents or hold a trump card over the head of an American diplomat. A man who had come to her six months before with a suitcase full of ready cash had known about her past and had even convinced her to risk her very freedom, not to mention her life....

Well, she had taken the money. There had been no choice really. The man seemed to know a lot about her past activities with the KGB, even had a list of former pigeons she had helped to pluck who just might want to speak to her again. The very image of the man, as she recalled him, made her shudder with revulsion. He was a bald man, his skin gray as ash, with dark, beady eyes—a walking skeleton in drab clothes.

She pushed any thoughts that might knock her off her present course out of her mind. She saw the senator waiting in the back, driver up front, engine running. The senator was all smiles, waving at her like some silly schoolboy. She was always surprised at how men of power and position were so easy to play when it came to a little extramarital sex.

It was definitely time to move on. She had just vacated her suite upstairs in the Rosslyn Marriott, the senator having put her up there since she'd made his intimate acquaintance. She would no longer need the room or the cad's token gifts and cheap jewelry. She'd no longer have to paint on an interested face during the wining and dining as he bragged about himself and his visions of a better America, which were naive to the point of absurdity. And, thankfully, she wouldn't have to hear all those empty promises he made about leaving his wife for her once his term was up, nor suffer through his feeble, clinging style of lovemaking.

But she didn't like the idea of riding this out to the end. The colonel had made it clear she couldn't walk until she was told she could. Yet there was the promise of more money, the kind of money that would let her call her own shots for the rest of her life.

He held open the door. She caught a whiff of his cologne, hated the fact that he seemed to think bathing in the stuff would make her want him like some cat in heat. She forced a smile to her face as she slid beside him, closing the door. She vaguely heard his opening monologue as she steeled herself, surprised in the next moment that she felt a tingle of excitement. She had never killed a man before, but something warned her that she had better live up to her end, or else.

She glanced at Robert Spellman's freshly scrubbed face. He was an older man, but there was nothing except a few gray hairs along the temples, not even lines around the eyes or mouth that tipped off he was well into his fifties. He reminded her more of some yuppie fresh out of college than a prominent political profile.

She took his hand, squeezed it, kissed him on the cheek. "I need to tell your driver something."

Then she heard the doors to the van close from beyond the car, knew they were on the march.

"Sure," he said, easy, rapping his knuckles on

the dividing glass. "Sounds mysterious, my little Czechi-Czechi."

"Not for long."

She pulled her hand away as the glass partition slid open. She reached inside her jacket, pulled out the 9 mm Makarov pistol with its sound suppressor. There was the usual bored look on the driver's haggard face until he saw the barrel coming up, inches from his eyes. His mouth opened but any sound that may have come out never made it as she stroked the trigger, putting a hole right between the driver's eyes. At point-blank range the slug blew an exit hole out the back of the driver's skull and cracked a spiderweb in the front windshield behind a thick spatter of crimson gore. She heard Spellman cry out, all shock and horror, then glimpsed a look on the senator's face that made her ill with contempt.

The man actually looked like was about to break out in a blubbery fit of begging. Then the doors burst open and Martika Kobeslav watched the senator jerk and spasm as he was hit by a stun gun. She jumped away from his twitching form, surprised by her own sudden loathing as she snarled, "Czechi-Czechi that, you asshole."

8

The Executioner was nearly forced to go for broke, his Beretta tracking the Syrian, his finger taking up the slack on the trigger. A blink of an eye before Mustapha's Colt Python drew a bead on Bolan, the big American locked on, the Beretta's unwavering muzzle aimed for a shot right between the eyes.

"Don't do it."

Mustapha hesitated, beaten to the punch. Then Bolan read the frightened look of the cornered animal relighting a fire in the Syrian's eyes.

"You won't make it," Bolan warned.

Mustapha stared at the Beretta, considering his options, not yet a true believer.

"It's a losing hand, Mustapha."

"Who are you?"

"Drop the gun. I won't ask again."

Reluctantly, Mustapha pitched the Python, sending it clattering to his desk.

"I'm Agent Belasko from the United States Department of Justice. That's the first and last question I'll answer."

"So I heard you tell it out there."

Bolan was getting a bad read on Mustapha. It was

something in his belligerent stance, the wild anger in his eyes. Last, but certainly not least, there was the smell of fear on the man.

"If you heard all that, then what's with the gun?"

"I've had death threats," the lean, swarthy Mustapha said. "So, the problem I have was you storm-trooping in here, clearing out my people like you owned the place or were maybe hell-bent on something else."

"Don't sandbag me, Mustapha, that's thin." The Executioner kept the Beretta trained on the Syrian's face. "This is Q and A. If I don't like the answers you and I are going for a drive. Meaning you're closed for business for as long as I say."

"I've got a permit for the gun."

"I clearly identified myself. That's enough by itself for me to haul you in."

"Okay, I made a mistake." Mustapha held his hands out by his side, as if he was Mr. Cooperation all of a sudden. "What do you want? I'm busy."

"You sold five properties in one day, about six months ago. It was a clean sweep, a fat payday for you and Hastings. Turns out your realty people were laundering money. Hastings Realty no longer exists, but that's just for starters."

"I already know that, I can read a newspaper. How was I supposed to know what they were doing? I'm not their bookkeeper."

"You sold one of your homes to an employee."

"The one to Ben Cross? I fired him two weeks ago."

"From what I know, that strikes me as a little too convenient."

"Convenient? The guy was a lush. He got so he couldn't even screw in a lightbulb much less wire up a high-tech security system. You're here to talk about a real estate deal, an ex-employee? Hey, if you've got a problem with Cross, go see him."

The Syrian was trying to brazen it out. And the more Bolan stared into the man's dark eyes the more he sensed Mustapha was willing to defy him until the end.

"About a year ago," Bolan said, putting Kurtzman's intel on the table, then moving to scoop up the Colt Python, "you attempted to get a passport and visa for your brother in Damascus, along with your two cousins."

The Syrian's gaze flickered off Bolan, and the soldier could see the wheels spinning, groping for a lie. "And?"

"The FBI nailed them as terrorists. They never made the flight here. They were picked up in Tel Aviv and handed over to the Israeli Mossad. It seemed they liked to blow up people, places and things on the West Bank. They've been rotting in an Israeli jail since."

"Your FBI cleared me on that."

"Maybe. How's this for Act Two? Five suspected terrorists were found in the house you sold to Cross."

"Terrorists? What the hell are you talking about?"

"They're no longer an issue." Bolan answered the Syrian's puzzled looked, saying, "Let's just say they were stamped for permanent deportation. Which leads me back to your Damascus problem. Tell me about your brother and your cousins. Why were you trying to get them into America?"

As Bolan opened his coat, then picked up and tucked the Colt Python inside his waistband, he saw Mustapha look pointedly at the Desert Eagle.

"That's a Fed's gun?" Mustapha grunted, suspicious.

"What did I say about the questions?"

"That's it," Mustapha growled, "game's over. I want to see some ID. I want to speak to your superior."

Bolan clenched his jaw. He was going to get nothing but lip service, a snow job. The Syrian was determined to dance him through a long day. Fair enough, Bolan could be very accommodating.

The Executioner flashed his Justice Department credentials in the Syrian's face, then made it disappear just as quickly.

"Have it your way," Bolan said as he reached out, fisted a handful of shirtfront and hauled the Syrian from behind his desk.

"What are you doing? Am I under arrest? Is this how a legitimate United States citizen is treated by the Feds?"

Bolan jacked Mustapha toward the door. "I understand. You have rights."

"Yes, I do, you bastard!"

If Mustapha had been afraid before he was now suddenly panicked. The Syrian wrenched himself out of Bolan's grasp, wheeled, almost caught the Executioner off guard. It was a short looping roundhouse punch and Bolan barely made it under the flying knuckles. Bolan had all the incentive he needed right then to jackhammer his fist deep into Mustapha's stomach.

The Executioner listened to the man suck wind and sputter profanities as he manhandled the Syrian out of his office. "You know, I was in a bad mood before I even laid eyes on you. Now I'm feeling downright hostile."

Bolan put some of that bad feeling into the shove he gave the Syrian across the outer office.

The Executioner was worried more than ever, his gut telling him something was going down, that a small army of international terrorists had invaded America, unless he missed his guess. They might have pulled up stake like thieves in the night, regrouped and relocated, but Bolan could feel them out there somewhere, moving in and ready to unleash some agenda of terror. But where were his enemies, and what did they intend to do?

There were so many unanswered questions, with nothing clearly defined about the opposition's agenda. This time out the Executioner had to concede his enemies had jump-started the program.

But finally, the Executioner had someone who could provide some answers.

FAROUK MALAKOUTI found his target just as it was was laid out during the dozen or so briefings by their American sponsors.

The National Air and Space Museum.

The short, stocky Iranian with his neatly trimmed beard and closely cropped black hair strolled right through the doors on the Independence Avenue side of the massive white stone building. Just like the colonel had promised, security was loose. No metal detectors or X-ray machines, no armed guards sizing everyone up, braced for trouble. In fact, the uniformed guards he saw carried nothing except a radio, handcuffs and pepper spray, most of them lumbering aimlessly or sitting, all of them looking bored. Easy work, but they would only mark the beginning. Malakouti smiled to himself, pleased that it was so far so good. What did the Americans say?

Like taking candy from a baby, yes, that was it.

Malakouti even liked the style of his American sponsors, all the code phrases and passwords that held the same militant contempt and hatred he had always carried in his heart for the Great Satan. This would, he thought, indeed be Allah's will.

He checked his watch. Exactly 1400. A bright, sunny day in the nation's capital, business as usual for his hated enemies.

He gave the plan for the massive takedown brief reflection, marveling for a moment at the sheer boldness of their sponsors' plan, but also forced to wonder what it was the Americans wanted out of this.

Forget it, he was long since committed to the plan.

Malakouti and twenty others were the spearhead for the bulk of troops. They were ordered to move inside the building in twos or threes, prepared to pave the way in just under one hour. There were twenty-three galleries in all, a lot of ground to seize, and that didn't include the three elevators, first-and second-floor bathrooms and third-floor staff office. The sprawling first and second floors where entire roving mobs of his enemies were gawking, with kids in tow, no less.

Stick with the plan, he told himself. Brute force, the sheer power of terror, and men with guns and grenades and the will to use them would get it started. Then appointed teams would seal all exits with plastique, while the rest herded the infidels at gunpoint. He envisioned mass groups of quivering infidel flesh, on their knees, begging for their lives while he showed them what a warrior who was right with Allah could do with the power of fear and a gun in his hand. Of course, he might have to kill a few of them, just to put the others in line. Some amount of killing, though, was expected, and his sponsors had granted as much. It was the rounding up and subduing of hostages that would turn the tide in their favor. If at all possible, they were ordered not to kill any women or children. If that happened Malakouti feared it would be over before it even got started. Maybe the entire wrath of the United States military would come crashing through the doors or down through the ceiling, weapons blazing, plastic explosive or not, hostages or no hostages.

He steeled himself, not caring to dwell on everything that could go wrong. He was in and moving, and his brothers-in-arms would be doing the same. As show for the general public, they carried tote bags over their shoulders and cameras. Fall in with the milling tourists, ride out the hour, do all the requisite "oohing" and "aahing."

Malakouti tugged the luggage-style carryall full of weaponry higher on his shoulder. He felt his blood running hot all of a sudden, his heart pounding with raw determination to begin hurling hell on earth into the faces of the infidels.

The camera looped around his neck, dangled down his chest as he fell in beside Musif Kharmouni. He couldn't resist smiling at his brother-in-arms. They had, indeed, come a long way since the war against Iraq, where another horde of enemies had been armed and aided by the United States. Back then Saddam Hussein had plenty of oil to sell, and where there was oil there were the Americans rushing in, offering all manner of promises and hope for the future. Well, if there was some divine justice in the fact that Hussein had eventually turned on the Americans, biting the hand that feeds, then Malakouti believed it was simply a blessing by Allah for the long haul.

Walking past the Staff Only escalator that led downstairs, Malakouti searched the lobby over by the Jefferson Street doors. Biltman was just now rolling in, satchel and camera in place. Looking around, smiling, Biltman was just another tourist. It was an encouraging sight, but Malakouti had never thought that the Americans were setting them up, prepared to bail and leave them eating dung at the doomsday hour. No, they wanted something from their own, and by way of blood. Whether it was money or to make some statement to America, Malakouti wasn't sure. It only mattered that he was ready to act.

The Iranian checked his flanks and melted into the crowds. He searched the faces of the tourists around him, and felt fire come alive in his belly. They looked so childlike, even naive in their sense of freedom, their fast-food bodies made soft and slow—another trapping of their obscene wealth, he reasoned—their eyes dulled, perhaps from minds numbed by the illusion of personal safety and security, a gift bestowed on them by their government.

Power, money and comfort. Safety, security, the pursuit of happiness and the indulgence of pleasure. They made him sick with hate. He concluded they had everything denied him in his own country, but through no real fault of his own.

What would his life matter anyway, if he couldn't take his revenge against those who kept his own people down and poor, forgotten at best, enslaved to the Great Satan at worst, as they eked out a beggar's existence?

Yes, it would be vindication for all Islamic peoples everywhere for him to see pure terror wipe away the contentment on those faces.

Allah was just, after all. Allah would see justice done.

A look to the right and Malakouti saw Biltman strolling toward the lunar modules and the rockets, the man merging with his fellow Americans. It was a go, all they had to do was ride out the time. The pager in his pants pocket would vibrate with the signal to get it started.

Malakouti walked for the museum gift shop. He looked at his watch again, silently cursed the excruciatingly slow passage of time. Only two minutes had passed since he had entered the museum.

Hold on, keep heart. Soon, very soon, he thought, and chuckled to himself, they would make their own stand against the Great Satan. Even if they were forced to go out as martyrs in the jihad, fighting alongside Americans, no less, they would turn this hallowed institution into the National Air and Space Mausoleum.

IT WAS A SHAME, perhaps even a slap in the face, Kamil al-Ashada thought. A city the size of Washington, bulging with thousands of potential targets, infidels swarming everywhere—five million according to the last census and his own brief—and he was assigned the Orange Line on the Metro.

Long before he was recruited, trained and smuggled into America, the Syrian had seen himself going out in glory with a suicide charge up the steps to the Capitol building. There he was, loaded down with high-explosives, pressing the button and taking out hundreds of infidels, not to mention more than a few of their leaders in a fireball he would ride straight to the bosom of Allah. Or maybe he would blow himself up as a gaggle of tourists stood in line to get into the Washington Monument, maybe wait until he was at the top setting himself off, taking out the pencil-tip pinnacle, while flinging himself and dozens of the devils clear to the Reflecting Pool.

So many targets, so few warriors in the jihad to get it done right. Pitiful.

All things considered, maybe he wasn't settling for second best. As he looked at the commuters packed shoulder to shoulder, all of them avoiding eye contact with one another, some with noses pressed into newspapers or paperbacks, one or two of them with headphones attached to radios, he felt the hate burn from deep inside his belly. They were sheep, doing what was expected of them.

A train car packed with human sheep, he finally concluded, and all of them being led to slaughter.

He had gotten on at the Vienna station, lugging the duffel bag with its eighty-pound payload. Everything was packed, wired for one radio signal. Fortunately he had found a seat alone near the back of the car and beside his exit door. He now sat behind a glass partition where the duffel bag was spread out by his feet, enough bulk hopefully to discourage anyone from sitting next to him.

The car was swelling with commuters who had

piled in at the Ballston and Courthouse stops. A few of them glanced his way, maybe wanting to drop down next to him, but they seemed to silently weigh the trouble it would take to have him slide the bag over.

Rosslyn was the next stop, the transfer to the Blue Line. Two days before, he had made the dry run, as ordered. At that time of day the platform would be packed with the workforce trying to beat rush hour. The crush of flesh would shave his escape close. He would work with that, he had to.

He checked his watch, ran his tongue over suddenly dry lips and felt a bead of cold sweat roll down his neck. In roughly five minutes the war against the Great Satan would begin. He had to get off the train, up the escalator and out into the street, then link up with a fellow soldier who had his own duty and their escape route mapped out. From there it was anybody's guess what would happen. He really didn't care about the future, other than seeing his part in the war come to blazing and glorious fruition.

He heard the driver announce the Rosslyn stop, a voice that jolted him to grim reality. His heart felt like a jackhammer in his chest as the train slowed, then stopped. They were packed by the door, unmovable objects, their jammed presence making him silently curse. He would have to excuse himself profusely just to clear it and get out on his way. And that would have to be done according to how he timed leaving his seat and package, then clearing the door just as it closed.

The doors opened. People surged in and out.

He waited a full second then rose from his seat. Head bowed, he shouldered his way through the commuters mumbling, "Excuse me, please."

Then he heard it, a voice calling out that chilled him to the bone, made his pulse race even faster, before a strange heat fired his brain with fear. He was moving through the doors when he heard, "Hey, mister, you forgot your bag. Mister?"

He was tempted to look back but hastened his stride, relieved when he heard the doors chime then shut. A moment later the train was rolling, the tunnel full of rumbling metal and the rush of wind.

Now he chanced a look over his shoulder, saw the squeeze of confused faces hovering near the seat he'd vacated, two men staring down at the duffel bag, one of them even reaching for it. It was actually going to happen, he was about to win his seat in paradise.

A sea of faceless bodies surged around him on the platform when he reached into his coat pocket, found the small box and flipped the switch.

It was activated. "For the glory of Allah."

He glimpsed the train gathering speed for the tunnel, the last car passing out of sight, then he gathered his own momentum, hit the escalators and thumbed the button. He was moving up the steps, climbing fast, light on his feet when the explosion shook the air. It was a peal so long and loud and tremendous he thought the walls would come down on his head in an avalanche of concrete and steel, bury him before he could manage another step. There was so much thunder, clanging of metal and screaming that he couldn't even absorb the terror of the moment. No, the thought corrected him, the beauty of the moment.

Keep climbing, pump the legs, make the street. He felt the terrible heat racing up the escalator below. This was his moment of victory, something he had only dreamed about all of his life.

Kamil al-Ashada was hitting the sidewalk in front of the metro station when he heard another ear-shattering blast. It was more sweet music to his ears.

He looked to his right and smiled at the sight of the fireball climbing up the side of the Gannett building. That would be his partner, one of the UPS truck drivers.

The smile vanished as he was forced to cover his head. Glass and other debris rained over the street, his ears once again pummeled by cries of terror and pain coming at him from all directions.

It kept raining wreckage for long moments, the fireball shooting up the building that housed the *USA Today* newspaper. The explosion was blowing in the windows, he knew, consuming anyone sitting in those offices in a raging mushroom cloud of flames.

Kamil al-Ashada laughed out loud as people screamed and dropped all over the street, crying out in their pain and horror as they were pelted by debris.

The war against the Great Satan had begun.

9

Hal Brognola was getting angrier and more frustrated with each lingering hour of ignorance and inaction. The big Fed stood by his office window watching the street below, seeing but not registering the flurry of activity. His tired mind had been flayed by so many unanswered questions, so much mystery, he now figured to just ride out the splitting headache brought on by what he silently called his ghost problem. Maybe more stress and discomfort would jar loose some answer he knew roiled around the jackhammer behind his eyes.

He stared out the window, jaws clenched. The bulk of the late lunch crowd was now heading back to work. The Justice Department was one of four mammoth buildings that made up the federal triangle. It was a vital block in the nation's capital.

Brognola was exhausted. The past few days his office was his home around-the-clock. He couldn't even remember the last time he had a square meal, much less talked to his wife. Damn it! They had nothing legitimate to run with, other than background intel on twelve Special Forces soldiers gone MIA and a renegade CIA operative who was known as the Butcher and who liked to carve up his victims. Not much to work with by a long shot. The bottom line was they were simply dancing with shadows, hungrily waiting for a break, something to give, fearing the worst—whatever it was—and dreading it would all unfold too late to stop it.

Not even Striker—after putting Mustapha up in a motel in Fairfax—had come up with anything solid. So far the Syrian had clammed up. At first, Brognola recalled, he and Bolan had toyed with the idea of blindfolding Mustapha, then whisking him out to the Farm and sitting on him there, sweating him out until he cracked and gave them something to run with. But the Syrian was, at least on the surface, a legitimate and law-abiding citizen. A definite problem if the Syrian held his ground and stonewalled Bolan. And not even Brognola, with all his power and free rein handed him by the President, would cater to the idea of snatching citizens off the streets of America on a suspicious whim. But Mustapha had made Bolan believe in his guilt. For the moment that was good enough for Brognola. Why had the Syrian pulled a gun on Striker if he was such a good citizen? Then he had taken a swing at Bolan, and all this after Striker clearly identified himself as an agent for the U.S. Justice Department. It was thin, all things considered, holding Mustapha on attempted assault. It wouldn't play out in any court of law, perhaps, but it was enough to keep Bolan dangling threats over the Syrian's head just the same. Brognola knew Bolan was prepared to turn up the heat on Mustapha. The soldier was a master at psychological warfare, and God only knew, Brognola thought, what he could throw Mustapha's way to get the man to say something, anything about the possibility of a mass terrorist attack on U.S. soil.

If there was even anything to be learned from Mustapha.

Brognola was giving the street another surveillance. He watched a UPS truck drive slowly on, then double-park on the other side of the street, a good half block down. The hazard lights started flashing, then the familiar brown uniform of the UPS driver popped into Brognola's sight.

He watched for another moment as the driver, clipboard in hand, began a hasty beeline from the truck. Brognola was curious as to why the driver was nearly running—away from the Justice Department building.

Brognola finally decided it was nothing; warned himself to be careful of his thoughts. Chalk it up to more tension, the phantom terrorists in his mind.

He was turning and walking away from his window when he heard the explosion. The next thing Hal Brognola knew he was hitting the floor on pure instinct for self-preservation as his reinforced office window went hurtling in lethal fragments over his head.

ABI MUMRAK had gotten lucky to find a seat in the back of the bus to himself. It didn't matter that he'd done his homework, riding out the dry run that would drop him off at the appointed time and place. That was practice.

Now it was real.

For the past six months he and his roommate lugged in suitcases, steamer trunks and cardboard boxes into their apartment. Moving in, settling down, just two more immigrants swelling an already swollen immigrant population in Arlington County, Virginia. Who would even notice, much less care?

Only what they brought to the apartment was a thousand pounds of plastic explosive, slogged in fifty to a hundred pounds at a time. Six months, pretty much, to wire it all to one radio frequency.

The mission was a go but it was far from being a lock.

The abandoned apartment was now emptied of seventy pounds of plastique, which was primed in the duffel bag at his feet.

In less than a minute the bus would roll to his stop.

Mumrak got busy. He glanced up the aisle, counted maybe twenty passengers. The bus driver and other passengers stared ahead, having no idea what was about to happen.

Mumrak bent down, slid the second skin off the duffel bag. With fingers trembling, aware of the adrenaline burning through him, the sweat breaking out on his forehead, Mumrak unsnapped the slender folding metal rods in the second skin. They bulked the bag some, but it still looked like a deflating balloon. But it wouldn't look like he was walking off empty-handed if the bus driver turned some attention his way. Move with some haste, but calm and assured, and don't look anybody in the eye. That was one part of his training at the hands of his American sponsors. Less than a minute and counting, and he could feel his nerves turning into electrical charges.

He saw Vencor Hospital coming into view and checked his watch again. Right on time. At that moment it was either on the verge of starting or had already begun. He pulled the overhead cord, chiming the driver to stop. Now for his contribution.

Abi Mumrak stood, keeping the flabby duffel low by his side, away from any lingering scrutiny by the driver. Swiftly he moved down into the well as the bus jerked to a halt on squealing brakes. This was it, he told himself, his blood racing like fire in his veins, this was his personal day of retribution for being denied by America everything that country took for granted.

As he pushed open the doors and stepped out onto the sidewalk, clear and free, he heaved a sigh of relief. Then he experienced a deep flush of gratitude toward the American sponsors who had made all this possible. Allah did, indeed, work in mysterious ways.

The thought burned through his mind that after today he would no longer have to clean up other people's garbage, suffer through all the expected bowing and scraping, the humiliation he had endured at the hands of a people he naturally despised.

He was a free man, after six months as a slave in America, and he was making his own statement, a middle-finger salute to the Great Satan in the name of all oppressed Islamic peoples. Someday he might be able to return to his homeland, a conquering hero.

Abi Mumrak began walking in the opposite direction down Carlin Springs Road as the bus belched exhaust and rumbled on. He picked up his pace, reached into his pocket and pulled out the small black box.

He flicked the switch as he'd been taught by the Americans, sucked in a breath to steel his nerve, then depressed the button with his thumb. He had envisioned the explosion the night before in his dreams. It had been a fireball, bright and glorious as the sun, shooting over where he stood his ground, tall and proud, his eyes absorbing the blast, his very soul drunk on his own power.

In reality it was quite the opposite.

The entire bus was lost in a blinding mushroom cloud that puked it out, vaporized, sending huge jagged metal teeth flying in all directions. The shock wave was so great it knocked Mumrak off his feet. For a second he believed he was killed by the blast, unable to hear or see right away. His entire body felt ripped apart by the noise alone. Then he heard the wreckage pounding the road beside him.

He looked behind and saw mangled and bloody figures staggering from smoking wreckage up the street. Several victims collapsed on the sidewalk as burning debris kept raining from the sky. He thought he saw an old man stumbling along like a drunk minus an arm, but Mumrak was fighting to see straight and couldn't be sure of anything right then.

Mumrak gathered himself, stood and began jogging down the hill. His vision was clearing when he saw the smoke take to the sky from the direction of Columbia Pike. Right on time.

He couldn't stifle the laughter as he broke into a sprint. He had come to this country with hatred in his heart for everything the Great Satan stood for, determined to make his mark for the jihad, even if the hand that fed him belonged to infidels.

A mere busboy, he thought, who had made his fortune in the land of the free, the home of the brave, in blood and vengeance.

Welcome to America. He laughed to himself.

THE TRAIN lurched to a sudden stop in the tunnel. The driver's voice came over the intercom, a nervous edge to his words. Right away Mohammed Balbek knew exactly what was happening.

"Ladies and gentlemen, I'm going to have ask all passengers to get off at the next stop, Metro Center..."

Balbek searched the confused and worried faces of passengers squeezed in around him, heard their babble of questions as the driver stated something about an emergency situation, for everyone to please stay calm at this time.

The message was loud and clear to Balbek. The

war had begun, and his enemies were taking steps to fight back.

It was a pity his life was about to end, but he was long since committed to martyrdom. No, Balbek didn't mind going out as a martyr for the cause; it was expected, after all. Indeed, it was even longed for, a badge of honor in the Islamic world that saw America and its allies as a poisonous serpent that wouldn't rest until every last Muslim man, woman and child was either dead, subjugated or enslaved to its demonic will. He had lived his entire twenty-five years in search of the opportunity to take out as many of his enemies as possible while giving glory to Allah with the sacrifice of his own life. Not even the knowledge of his own coming death would deny him his right to vengeance, to glory.

Balbek reached down, unzipped the duffel bag and hauled out the mini-Uzi. It was already locked and loaded, so all he had to do was squeeze the trigger. He did.

Terror and chaos erupted instantly the second the compact SMG flamed and stuttered. His opening rounds blew through the backsides of several men and women in front of him, pitching them in tangled heaps against the door. At the top of his lungs he screamed, "Death to America! Death to the Great Satan!"

He spun, firing, watching his victims trample each other to get out of his line of bullets. He held back on the trigger, their shrieks of horror and cries of agony only fueling his hatred and resolve. Blood spattered his face as he hosed them at point-blank range. They kept screaming, scrambling up the aisle or attempting to hide behind their seats even as he sprayed bullets into their backs. Pivoting, he caught one man flush in the chest with a short burst as the American charged him—only to become a dead hero.

The clip would burn up in a few seconds, he knew, so he pulled the small black box from his coat pocket, activated the signal to the plastic charge.

He heard someone scream, "He's got a bomb! Oh, my God! He's got a bomb!"

There were shouts to grab him, everything suddenly in slow motion in his sight as he dredged up the resolve to do it.

"Death to America!"

It was the last thing Mohammed Balbek heard as he hit the button and put the final touch on his destiny.

THEY WOULD NEVER leave Tyson's Corner mall alive but Hamid al-Masouk didn't care. In war personal sacrifices were necessary if the greater good of the righteous Islamic warrior was to be furthered. And they were at war, make no mistake.

As he rolled into the department store with the satchel of grenades and spare clips slung over his shoulder for his Ingram MAC-10, he palmed the Russian F-1 grenade and gave Talibaba the nod. Going in he had hit the button on his beeper, sending out the vibrating signal. At the lower level and on the opposite end of the mall he knew the other half of his holy team was hard at work.

Together they pulled the pins and pitched the grenades far away, dropping the steel eggs into the glass rings of counters where women sold jewelry and perfume. Even at a safe distance, outside the radius of the danger zone, the twin blasts were deafening. It was only a blur, caught out of the corner of his eye, but the explosions spewing out countless steel fragments sent torn bodies flying in all directions. With glass and heat blowing around the department store, he felt as if he was standing in the eye of a hurricane. He slitted his gaze and walked boldly on.

The Syrians pulled their Ingram MAC-10s from the special shoulder rigging beneath their topcoats.

It wouldn't be long, Hamid al-Masouk knew, before all the law that Fairfax County could marshal would surround and storm this rich playground of his enemies.

He ignored the frenzied cries of horror all around him, and held back on the SMG's trigger. There were plenty of targets. Going in he had prayed to take out at least one hundred shoppers before he had to face the police and go out in glory.

One hundred victims by his own hand was a nice round number to Hamid al-Masouk.

He could die with that.

BROGNOLA IGNORED the blood streaming down his face from the cuts on his scalp. Somehow he had made his way out of the building and onto the street. He had been dazed, at first, urging his legs to move, get outside and see if there were wounded he could tend to.

Cold rage then swept over him as he saw the carnage strewed before him. Nothing moved, nothing stirred, not even a lone cry of misery. He had his Glock 17 out, fanning the smoke cloud that boiled across the street over the dead. For what little good it would do, he was searching for a target, hoping against hope to see and nail the murdering bastard who had created the horror he now witnessed.

No such luck. The bogus UPS driver was long gone.

Hal Brognola had seen plenty of death and destruction in his time, knew exactly the kind of justice Bolan and the other Stony Man warriors meted out to the cannibals of the innocent. That was different because it was war against armed opponents, against men who wanted nothing other than to inflict their violence and their will on combatant and noncombatant alike.

What he now viewed, stunned and sickened to the core of his soul, would boggle the mind of the most battle-hardened of soldiers.

This was mass, indiscriminate murder.

Brognola staggered on, in his nose the acrid smell of blood and leaking gas from the pulverized heaps of parked cars. The wail of sirens cracked through the ringing in his ears. They came running from all directions now, FBI and Justice Department agents swarming over the slaughter. Blue-and-whites came racing around the corner, lights on and sirens screaming, brakes screeching, squad cars disgorging uniformed policemen, who froze at what they saw.

Shaking, Brognola dropped a hand over the cellular phone clipped to his belt. Somehow it had stayed in place.

Brognola took the phone and began punching in the numbers to reach Mack Bolan.

War, Hal Brognola knew, had just been declared on America.

COLONEL BECKER was working his handheld radio fast and furious, taking sitreps from his key people inside, signing off and on with no more than two or three words per contact.

It was happening; the whole damn city was going up in flames. It was time to turn it up a few notches.

As soon as his miniconvoy of three oversize vans had begun the final leg down Jefferson Street, Becker had sent out the vibrating signal from his beeper. Now he could clearly see all hell had broken loose inside the National Air and Space Museum. People were streaming out the doors, a few panicked tourists even tumbling down the steps, all arms and legs and screams. It was a stampede that could hinder his own progress.

Becker feared they may lose the moment before they could seize it.

Edward Vinyard hit the brakes, sliding to a stop on the other side of Jefferson. The motorcycle cops by the concession stand were already off their bikes, grabbing radios, reaching for side arms.

"Go, go, go!" Becker shouted, slinging his SMG around his shoulder, then throwing open his door and shouting to the three cops, throwing in a little profanity to make sure he got their attention.

He got it. Becker and Vinyard hit the pavement, already pulling out their Colt pistols and drawing target acquisition, when the policemen wheeled around. Becker glimpsed his three ten-man teams in place with their Heckler and Koch MP-5 SMGs poised to fire. They were fanning out, human bolts of lightning, and he wished them well to get them all inside, safe and sound, on track.

The cops hesitated at the sight of a small heavily armed black-clad army surging at them. Becker and Vinyard didn't waste a heartbeat, firing rounds in tandem. Standard operating procedure was to go for head shots, since body armor was becoming regular issue in a city where the criminals had heavier firepower than the cops. Scoring, Becker and Vinyard charged on, leaving the bike cops twitching in their own blood and shattered skulls.

The mob kept barreling out the doors, but Becker had anticipated a general stampede once the bullets and tear gas were lobbed in the bathrooms and designated galleries that were too large to clear out without having to resort to mass extermination.

Becker needed hostages, and plenty of them, if he was going to pull it off.

He bounded up the steps, holstering his side arm

then unslinging his Heckler & Koch MP-5 submachine gun. All the shooting and screaming he heard from inside told him he was about to move into hell on earth.

It was only the beginning. And Becker wanted to believe the best was yet to come.

10

Phantom Alpha Six was inside, but getting the National Air and Space Museum under complete control was the next order of business. Becker took charge, immediately barking out orders to secure the hostages first. They had a toehold, but they needed the strangle. There could be no relaxing, no backing off now, and orders had to be followed to the letter. The cavalry was sure to be on the way. Becker needed the building seized, hostages down and explosives positioned at all exits.

He was through the door, SMG poised to fire. He saw his teams spreading out, firing toward the ceiling for effect, his men shouting and cursing at the mob of tourists who were trying to beat a panicked flight for Jefferson and Independence. Within seconds most of the tourists were swarming the main lobbies on both sides, everyone ordered to hit their knees. A few tough guys had to be clipped over the head or beaten into submission. But Becker expected some resistance, hell, he would have been disappointed in the American fighting spirit if all of them had been herded, meek as lambs.

They became more puppet than human to Becker,

pure terror carved into their faces, shocked expressions staring back at him. They were pawns on his chessboard anyway and he would use them however he saw fit to get what he wanted, eventually to see his people clear and free. Easier imagined, of course, but they were in the thick of it, locked in.

The noise roared around Becker in the sprawling complex. It was maddening in its relentless swirling din, but seemed to urge all of them on, he proudly saw. Get it done, use brute force, take no crap. Failure was unacceptable.

Women cried and screamed, men cursed and begged for the lives of their families to be spared. It ate up critical seconds, but Becker and his men had to reassure the civilians—under the muzzles of their SMGs—that no one would be shot if they did as they were told.

Then Becker saw an old man in a *USS Hornet* cap coming at him, all snarls and wild eyes.

"Don't do it, pop!" Becker roared at the old sailor. The old guy charged him anyway. Dumb ass swabbie, he raged to himself. Becker was forced to lay him out with a 3-round burst to his chest. The wife shrieked as he dropped over the body of her dead spouse. Then an SMG-wielding Arab wrenched her up by her hair and tossed her into a kneeling pack of tourists, cursing the woman in his native tongue. Becker didn't really care for the amount of force or the verbal humiliation the Arab used on the woman.

Indiscriminate killing and gratuitous brutality,

though, could pose a problem, the colonel knew. Over the years in remote desert regions in Syria and across North Africa he had trained the Muslim contingent for this very day. He was well aware of their hatred for anything of the West. Even still, they had pledged allegiance to Becker. It helped that he had put a few bucks in their pockets, with the promise of more money when the job was done. He had strung them along even more, vowing safe passage to a country in the Middle East where he would use his connections to get them all situated and create a global network where they could carry on their jihad. Of course, that was then, now was now and tomorrow was always in doubt.

So the next problem he might have to tackle may be overzealousness of the Arabs. Already the lobbies and hall on both sides of Becker were littered with corpses. Mostly museum guards, he saw, but some tourists had gone down, either dead heroes or outright sacrifices to make a point. At this juncture Becker could only hope his Arab force didn't go berserk, unleash all that hate and rage and start mowing down women and children. If they did, well, Becker would have to volunteer one or two of them as examples.

The screaming and the crushing swarm of bodies moved toward Becker as he rolled left and marched for the Rocket and Space hall. It was a constant jolt to the senses. Marching on, he smelled blood and the bitter taint where tear gas had been used in the first- and second-floor bathrooms and several of the galleries. Above, from the second floor, he made out the gagging and choking, the hacking pleas for mercy, followed by a few more staccato bursts of subgun fire.

Becker gave the order to begin the mining but was pleased to see the demolition teams were already laying out the blocks of C-4 along the base of all the doors. Already Weathers and Kurchin were rolling for the Air Transportation hall to take the roof. Coming down both winding staircases at each end, the tourists were being marched at gunpoint to the first floor. A few of them lost their legs or were shoved hard by a few overenthusiastic Arabs and tumbled down the steps.

Vinyard had hauled out the radio backpack right on cue and was now moving to help set up the command center near the special aircraft exhibits.

Becker got on the handheld for a sitrep. He radioed each key team. They reported all clear. Third-floor offices were seized and personnel neutralized. The elevators were taken down, blown up into useless steel boxes so no one could come up from below. Parking garage doors were mined and patrolled. All communications were destroyed. Working on the galleries still, flushing tourists out, Artillon reported he had to wax a couple of wanna-be heroes but they were nailing the rooms down. Finally he reached the colonel who reported it was just about a wrap on the second floor, galleries and theater. The visiting team was rolling ahead, no problems on Biltman's end.

Victory was in sight, Becker sensed, but this was only one battle.

Then a double explosion rocked the air far to his right flank. Moving back past the main doors, Becker watched as the smoke cleared above the suspended Douglas DC-3 airplane. That would be Weathers and Kurchin, having just blasted through the ceiling skylight with 40 mm grenades launched from their M-16 M-203 combos. They were already scrambling atop the Douglas DC-3, grappling hooks hurled through the smoke to catch a bar somewhere beyond the jagged glass. Next a minisatellite-radar dish would go out on the roof. There were four main sections on the roof and Becker would position eight snipers up top—four facing down Jefferson, four overlooking Independence. Equipment and the heavier explosives, he saw, were already being handed over to his men on the big plane.

Clockwork. He allowed himself to indulge in a moment of amazement at how fast and efficient his people had operated. Whatever the Arab terrorists lacked in training they made up for with desire.

Then the expected problem reared up. Becker saw the squad cars lurching all over the place on Jefferson, turned and saw the flashing lights whipping into sight beyond the Independence doors. Uniformed cops took up positions, side arms and shotguns swinging into view.

"I need a wall along the doors on both sides, gentlemen," Becker told a group of Arabs. It was something they'd gone over during the countless briefings. They knew the drill and went to work, not missing a beat.

Naturally it took some encouragement with the butts of SMGs and a little firing over their heads, but in less than two minutes the Arabs had gathered thirty or so hostages for the bank of doors along each main entrance. The hostages now stood in front of the entrances, quaking in terror, a whimper or two breaking through all the shouting. Shoulder to shoulder, they were forced to press their noses into the glass, hands above their heads. They were told by the Arabs if they moved, if they dropped—either out of fear or exhaustion—they would be shot without hesitation.

Becker had his human wall.

It was time to address the nation.

MAX KELLY glanced at his watch, then took the remote control and snapped on the big-screen television. He muted the sound.

They were all gathered in the living room, with the exception of Scott who was monitoring the front of the house from an upstairs bedroom window.

The hostages were packed on the couch, all of them cuffed, hands behind their backs. Kelly measured each expression, more out of curiosity than concern they might come unhinged and make a grandstand charge. They were clearly afraid, but seemed resigned to their fate for the moment, if he was any judge of human nature under such duress. But the ex-Marine had sat there for hours in stony silence, Kelly feeling his angry stare the whole time, Senator Walker having given up on any dialogue after Kelly refused to answer his questions. Walker was a soldier's soldier, Kelly decided, and he would hate to have to waste an ex-Marine.

Kelly glanced over at Jamal and Fasrah. They had taken positions across the room, their SMGs low by their sides. Their eyes shone with something Kelly couldn't quite put his finger on. His Islamic partners clearly seemed to be enjoying the party. He kept waiting to hear their laughter and could imagine them breaking out the champagne.

It was show time, according to his watch. Kelly flipped around the stations. It was on every channel, but then nothing like this had ever happened in the history of America. Kelly could well imagine the horror that had gripped the land. It was the worst nightmare for the greatest military power, the strongest nation and the wealthiest country in the history of man. In the span of minutes, a few good men had created an anarchy that had shown the mighty just how weak and vulnerable they really were. Wait until the mighty, he thought, learned just what the price tag was for them to reclaim whatever respect and dignity and illusion of security they believed they could salvage.

Kelly watched the screen. Images of police vehicles, military choppers roving the skies over the Potomac River, reporters gesturing at ambulances or at the smoking facades of several buildings he recognized—all whipped by as he worked the remote.

Kelly kept going through the channels until he came to CNN.

"This may or may not put a few things into perspective, Senator," Kelly said.

The young, good-looking female reporter was clearly agitated. She flailed an arm behind her at the crush of police vehicles, fire engines, ambulances and the two MedStar choppers that were grounded on the street. Kelly recognized the area as the Rosslyn Metro station. He turned up the volume.

"It's like a war zone here, that's the only way I can think of to describe it. But it's a scene that this reporter, that none of us can even begin to describe much less comprehend." Her voice cracked and she seemed on the verge of losing it. Not very professional, Kelly thought, but listened as she sucked in a deep breath and went on, "I'll give it to you the best I can, but we've got reports coming in from all over..." She paused as she read something off the monitor. "I'm informed that there may have been as many as fifteen such terrorist attacks around the city and the suburbs. We can confirm ten. We have no report on casualties but we understand they are severe, and that the hospitals in the city and the outlying suburbs can't take care of all the wounded. We've just learned that the Army and the Marines have already been called in to secure and help evacuate the city and surrounding suburbs..." She touched her earpiece, a gesture that brought on a fresh look of shock and horror. "We understand looting has broken out in certain areas inside the city…''

Kelly moved to another channel. The handsome face of an older man with gray hair, sheaf of papers in hand, came on. He was standing along Route 7. Kelly recognized the backdrop of low-lying buildings that marked Tyson's Corner.

''We haven't been able to confirm the number of dead and wounded inside the mall but we do have confirmation that four terrorists—and at this point we are referring to them as terrorists, from what country, what they want, we don't know…''

Kelly smiled. The reporter talked at a rapid-fire pace, having obvious difficulty digesting the enormity of what he reported, stumbling over his thoughts and words, clueless, it seemed, but trying his damnedest to clue in America.

''…they were finally shot and killed as Fairfax County Police stormed inside…'' He touched his earpiece, heaved a sigh and looked pained. ''I've just been informed that perhaps as many as ten to fifteen police officers—that number is unconfirmed—were killed during what appears to have been a suicide assault by the terrorists. Unconfirmed reports indicate the terrorists used grenades…''

Kelly hit the mute button. He'd heard enough. He saw the rage build in the senator's eyes, the shock and horror drop like a veil over the faces of the wife, children and housekeeper. Fasrah and Jamal chuckled. They muttered something in Arabic, Kelly catching ''Allah'' during the exchange.

"Is that what this is all about?" Walker growled. "You people are terrorists?"

"Dear God, if what we just saw is happening…" Mrs. Walker fell silent, trembling.

"It's happening, ma'am," Kelly told her. "That's just a sample. And, sir, I've heard it told that one man's terrorist is another man's freedom fighter."

The wife looked at Kelly with revulsion. "You aren't any crusader, you aren't any freedom fighter, you sick animals. All those people…innocent people you…whoever you are have killed…"

"There are no innocents, Mrs. Walker," Kelly said, "That's what this is partly about. Hey, Senator, you're a former combat vet. I'm sure you can understand. We're at war here."

"I don't think I can or even want to understand a damn thing about you. I echo what my wife just said."

"Fair enough," Kelly said. "Here's the deal, boys and girls. This city now belongs to us, and you needn't trouble yourself figuring out who we are. It's not about ransom money, it's not about straightening out your political agenda."

Walker nodded, clenching his teeth so hard it looked as if he could chew bullets and spit them out. "We're bait."

"Not bait, sir, but our ticket to ride. A trump card, if you will. Before long, we may find out just how much your constituents value your seat in the senate, sir." Kelly lifted the remote control, glanced at his Arab partners then looked back at the hostages, smiling. "Now, why don't we sit back and watch some TV. Nothing like live entertainment."

Kelly got a laugh from Jamal and Fasrah.

IT WAS A SIEGE, total and complete, without question.

The impossible had happened. The worst-case scenario, which before had only been an idea kicked around and dreaded in the Pentagon and every U.S. Intelligence and law enforcement agency, had now become cold, terrifying reality.

Mack Bolan had one simple question for Hal Brognola. Where did they go from there? The answer was simple on the surface, at least in Bolan's mind. Somehow get to the bastards and crush them before any more innocent civilians were killed. Getting it done could prove extremely difficult if what the Executioner gleaned on his end from the current dialogue between Brognola and the President of the United States held up.

Bolan stood at somber attention in the big Fed's office. The door was closed, and the carpet around the soldier had remained an untouched bed of glass since the explosion. Beyond the shattered window, Bolan heard the sirens as well as the swirl of angry and frightened voices of cops and paramedics on the street below. Washington D.C., he knew, was under attack. Resources, both police and medical, were already stretched thin. The soldier feared they hadn't even seen the worst of it.

Brognola set down the secure phone to the Oval

Office. Blood still flowed down the big Fed's face but he refused any medical attention. There were a few survivors out on the street in front of the Justice Department building, and Brognola had already made it clear they needed medical attention far more than he did. The big Fed wasn't giving up his office either. This was war, he had told Bolan, and Brognola would stay in the trenches.

Bolan met Brognola's dazed stare. A few of the sirens faded, but the calls of panic and concern kept pouring through the broken window.

Finally Brognola stood, held his arms out by his side, his stare mirroring the fear and shock even Bolan felt.

"Why the National Air and Space Museum? It has absolutely no strategic importance, military, political or otherwise."

Bolan didn't say anything. He didn't really have the first clue as to why the enemy would choose such a landmark to take and hold hostages, but he could hazard a guess or two.

"Why?" Brognola repeated.

Bolan drew a deep breath. He willed away the rage he felt, knowing it would do no good to let anger get the best of him. A clear head, direction and action were called for.

"I'll venture a guess, Hal. I would say because it's a landmark, it's right in the thick of all the political institutions that count. We don't know what they have inside with them, or even in the immediate area."

"A nuke? Is that what you're thinking?"

"We don't know. The target they took down isn't exactly a fortress like all other federal buildings."

"Meaning security is lax and they selected it for that reason alone."

"We don't have any concrete answers at the moment, anything we say now is pure speculation. Who's on-site over there?" Bolan asked.

"The FBI. For the moment."

"We need to take charge, Hal. I want the President to be clear on this. No Rapid Response Teams, we want no obvious military presence near there until we find out what they want or until we decide how we're going to move on this."

"That was the Man just now, but you know that. I've been on the phone—where's that bastard, Mustapha?"

"I left him with two of your agents downstairs. So far, I've gotten nothing from him. He's dirty somehow, that's what my gut's telling me."

"Lean on his ass," Brognola snarled. "If he knows something, if he's involved, I want him broken..."

Bolan understood his friend's ire all too well but he needed to get some matters squared away. There would time enough later to rage and to mourn the dead.

"Later, Hal. He's not going anywhere. Right now we need to assess the situation and get a plan together."

"Yeah, a plan. Since I last talked to you, I haven't

been off the phone. My assistants, the President, the FBI, the Pentagon. Do you how many dead and wounded we're looking at?''

Bolan let Brognola go with it. The Executioner had some of the particulars. First reports had sixteen different terrorist attacks, in and around the city. Car bombings on the BW Parkway, the Beltway; terrorists setting off their vehicles in traffic, taking out as many commuters as possible in the suicide blasts. Three Metro lines were down, trains obliterated on the Orange, Red and Blue Lines. A bus had been blown apart in Arlington, along with half an apartment building just up the street. Gunmen strolled into Tyson's Corner and White Flint Mall and hurled grenades, mowing down countless shoppers with automatic weapons fire before going out in some warped blaze of glory at the guns of the police. That was only the shortlist. There were no firm numbers on dead or wounded, but the first figures, Bolan was now informed by Brognola, were reaching into the low thousands.

''I hear what you're saying, Striker. But the President is fighting all sides now. Every branch of the military, his cabinet, the Pentagon—it's a mess. The outrage is understandable on all fronts, as you can well appreciate.''

''We need clearance.''

''One chief, not a bunch of Indians hacking away at each other, I read you. Okay, the Man assured me he will pull executive privilege but he'll be dancing around all sorts of minefields. Stony Man's cover may end up being the last of his concerns, but I know he wants us on board and he's willing to go with whatever we decide." Brognola cursed. "He wants to know how this could have happened. He wants to know what he's going to tell the American people. He has to go on television in fifteen minutes and try to sort some kind of order out of this madness before the whole nation becomes unraveled and we're looking at armed revolt because the government can't protect its own citizens. We've got the National Guard, and hell, I can't even go over the list of Army and Marine personnel on the way, it's so many. There's already major looting in the city. There's not enough room in all the hospitals in the area for the wounded, so the Army is now setting up makeshift hospitals in the Virginia countryside." Brognola slammed his fist on his desk. "We are looking at a catastrophe, and I'm not even sure that's the right word."

The Executioner waited as his friend wiped some blood out of his eyes. The look of raw determination that fired Brognola's eyes told Bolan, if nothing else, that everyone from the Oval Office on down wanted the same thing. Right then there was the safety of countless hostages to weigh and consider. Beyond that, the Executioner knew it would come down to retribution, plain and simple.

"I want these bastards, Striker."

11

Colonel Becker decided to show them how much he liked kids. Slipping the H&K MP-5 over his shoulder, he pulled out the .45 ACP Colt pistol. Marching for the human wall, he picked a pudgy teenager for his shield. In one lightning motion, before the parents could squawk, Becker yanked the boy and barreled outside. With his arm locked around the boy's throat, he stuck the Colt's barrel into the kid's ear and thumbed back the hammer.

Walking toward the first set of steps, he felt the kid shaking in his grasp. "Just relax, son, and we'll both make it back inside."

The colonel watched as the cops and Feds readjusted their aim, shotguns racking, pistols cocking. Becker was staring down an army of uniformed city cops, and the unmarked vehicles with their dark-suited gunmen had to be FBI. All of them looked angry enough to unload at the next slightest provocation. Oh well, he figured. Life didn't mean squat unless there was risk—a warrior lived no other way. Right then he had all the adrenaline rush he could handle.

Becker stepped to the edge of the steps and

stopped. As he gave them all a once-over the colonel felt himself swell with angry pride. This was his show, he was in charge. No way would they just start blasting once they learned the score inside the museum. Of course it could go either way, but he felt more powerful than at any single moment in his life. Countless lives had been thrown into the hopper, and he could pull out who lived and who checked out. This was the ultimate in living on the edge, he thought. It was something far more euphoric than any drug on earth, any amount of sex, fame and fortune. Whatever, it was good to have lived long enough to feel a moment like this. Priceless, in fact.

A man in a suit lifted a bullhorn from behind an unmarked vehicle. "What is it you want?"

"Identify yourself."

"Special Agent Ross Morrow. FBI. Who am I speaking to?"

"God." Becker laughed. "You're speaking to God."

A few cops muttered oaths. Morrow gnashed his teeth as he lifted the bullhorn again and said, "Listen to me. You're surrounded, the Army is currently moving in to monitor your movement from above and they will drop the sky on you if you don't surrender immediately."

"Well, thank you for that piece of information, son. You're telling me a Rapid Response Team is en route?"

"You have no choice but to surrender."

Becker liked that. "Are you that stupid? Are you the one with the hostages? Did I miss something on the way out here?"

"Before this goes any further, I want any wounded inside the building to be removed."

"There are no wounded."

"You're telling me you've got a bunch of dead bodies in there? You bastard!"

"Let's just say the city has some bona fide deadweight but it's no longer at the taxpayer's expense," Becker responded.

"What do you want?"

"We'll get to that shortly. Here it is, asshole, the short and the sweet. First, the entire building, including all entrances, the elevator shafts, the parking garage, in short, any way in or out is mined with plastic explosive. We're monitoring all frequencies in the area, all airwaves are locked up and under our thumb, and that includes air traffic. If there is any movement against us, I won't hesitate to blow up this building. All you have to do is look around the city a little and you'll see I can deliver on my promise to bring this building down, along with the six or seven hundred tourists inside. You'll excuse me if I didn't have time to take an accurate head count for you."

"Cut the bullshit. What do you want?"

"All business, I like that. What I want right now, Mr. FBI, is a direct line to the President. I have a cellular phone and I will give you a number to give to him that I have already preset." Becker called out seven number sixes. "I know the line can be broken into. No problem. That way everyone, from his secretaries of propaganda and misuse of campaign funds on down to his Joint Chiefs of Clowns and you morons can listen in."

"Those numbers, you're joking, right?" the FBI man growled.

"You want to step inside for a minute and see if anybody's laughing? I didn't think so. The President has ten minutes to get on-line. Meanwhile you people have thirty seconds to clear these vehicles off the road. Back them up on the Mall, I don't care. Clear Independence Avenue of the city's finest while you're at it. If you don't obey my orders you're in for one nasty surprise and you can kiss your pension and your ass, Mr. FBI, goodbye. My personal bullet with your name on it, son, will look better in comparison."

Becker heard Weathers on his handheld radio. He put the gun in his other hand, hugging the kid tighter to his chest. With his free hand he unclipped the handheld and lifted it to his face, keeping the guns in sight. "Report."

"Colonel, we've got unfriendly skies. I'm looking at two sets of armed wings to the east, sir. Army birds."

Becker checked his watch. "Sync in, soldier. If they don't back off in thirty seconds, pick one and light it up."

"That's affirmative, sir. Over and out."

Becker raised Joe Artillon. "Get all hostages clear

of the doors now, down on the floor, well clear of the lobbies. Synchronize. Twenty-five seconds then light up Independence on my order. You copy?''

''Roger that, Colonel.''

The commotion behind Becker raised the tension on the street. Confused and angry faces stared past Becker. A new wave of terror roared from inside the museum.

''What the hell's going on in there?'' Agent Morrow rasped.

Becker heard the bleat of chopper blades beyond the building. ''I don't see you people moving! You've now got fifteen seconds to fall back!''

''Go! Everyone pull back to the Mall!'' Morrow ordered.

Guns disappeared.

''Ten seconds!''

They began piling into their vehicles, firing up engines. Becker decided some more incentive was called for. He fumbled around the boy, plucked a hand grenade, pulled the pin and released the spoon.

Becker pitched the grenade into the street, sending it bouncing under a squad car. It was a dud, which made their panic almost comical. It was all Becker could do to keep from laughing as they screeched out of there. Two squad cars slammed into each other, smashing headlights and dinging metal, then reversed and got it right as they followed the caravan out onto the Mall.

''We're clear in here, sir,'' Artillon reported.

A check of his watch. Five seconds and counting. He called Weathers, "Phantom Flyer, come in!"

"Phantom Flyer here, sir. They're hovering a little too close for comfort. I've got a lock on them with an Ivan. Give the arrogant pricks a taste, sir?"

"Fire at will." They were all on the same frequency, everyone knowing the score right away, no tripping along. Over his radio, Becker heard the screaming and cursing from inside as everyone cleared the lobbies. Whether or not Morrow had cleared Independence was no longer Becker's concern. It was time to make another statement.

Becker sidestepped away from the doors. He couldn't see the Ivan—the RPG-7 warhead—streak for it's target, but he heard the peal of thunder to the east, glanced up in time and saw the fireball roiling over the museum. Bingo. He roared over the handheld, "Artillon!"

"Artillon here, sir!"

"Light them up!"

Becker hurled the boy to the ground, covered him with his own body. On the other side of the building he heard the series of blasts as the vans filled with explosives went off. Then the Jefferson Avenue doors were hit by shrapnel that blew across the lobbies. The doors cracked and splintered but held. Even still, God help anything that was caught in the middle of that firestorm, Becker thought.

He snatched up the teenager who was now crying and hauled him through the door. They had all been shoved away from the lobbies, and a damn good thing for everyone concerned. Becker saw the doors along Independence were now nothing but gaping holes of jagged glass. Flaming wreckage was still pounding the street.

"Get my walls back!" Becker ordered, stepping around the corner.

The Arabs went to work hustling tourists back to form human barricades.

"Johnny! Johnny!"

Becker spotted the teen's mother and father. Both of the parents made an attempt to break free of their own circle. Both made it all of two steps when two Arabs clubbed them over the head with the butts of submachine guns. Marching the boy along, Becker deposited the boy beside his mother. She wept, ignoring the blood streaming down her face and clutched her son. The father looked set to leap to his feet and take his chances until a subgun was shoved at his face.

Becker walked up to one of the Arabs and snarled, "What's your name?"

The dark man squared his shoulders. "Issam."

Becker shot a steely look at both Arabs. "Do something like that again and I'll shoot you dead. Are we clear?"

Issam looked stunned, and Becker was forced to bark his question again. The Arabs nodded, but Becker could tell they didn't like it. Too bad. If he lost control of the troops now all, of them might as well march right outside and hand themselves over to a sure death sentence.

Becker moved toward command central, ignoring the fear and outrage around him. It was just about time to make his demands known. In a few minutes he would speak with the President of the United States. After that he would know if the price was right for all concerned.

ANOTHER VISION of hell waited for Bolan and Brognola.

The Executioner slid the Crown Vic to a stop near the Jefferson Street edge of the Mall, across from the west corner of the National Air and Space Museum. He was piling out, Brognola already through the passenger door, when the fireball floated out of sight on the far side of the hostage landmark. The soldier had also clearly heard another series of explosions hammering the building from the Independence Avenue front.

The Executioner stayed right beside Brognola as they swiftly moved up the line of squad cars and unmarked FBI vehicles. Pandemonium rained on the Mall. Bolan felt the wall of fear closing around him. Cops were on their radios, firing off angry questions at a machine-gun staccato clip. Agents in FBI jackets were on their own handhelds, looking nearly crazed with their own fear and anger. It was a ceaseless babble, the rule of chaos and confusion absolute and supreme.

Bolan knew they needed to take control of the situation. Their way was already paved. The President had radioed the FBI agent-in-charge and told him to hand over the reins to Brognola and the Justice Department. The Man was busy right then, Bolan suspected, throwing around all manner of no-questions-asked orders. But the Executioner's primary goal was to thrust into the middle of this disaster without the military throwing muscle his way. First and foremost Bolan wanted to make certain no more innocent lives were claimed by an enemy that had clearly shown it had no regard at all for human life.

Vengeance would follow.

Brognola seemed to know just whom he needed to speak to. The big Fed marched up to a whip-lean, dark-haired agent in an FBI jacket.

"Morrow?"

"Yeah?"

"What's the situation?"

The FBI man stood behind the open door to his vehicle, a handheld radio poised to his lips.

"You Brognola?"

"Yes."

Bolan listened to Morrow's situation report. It was grim. The three vans the enemy had emerged from on Independence Avenue had just blown up all to hell all over the street. An undetermined number of police officers were down at the moment. One of two OH-58 Kiowa choppers was also downed by a rocket fired from the northwest quadrant of the roof. Four Army personnel were believed dead. Sirens now wailed from all directions, and Morrow had to shout. He informed Brognola he had just ordered the other chopper to fall back. The terrorist had claimed the entire building was a powder keg of plastic explosive, wired to blow. It was as far as Morrow got. The FBI man became a study in rage.

"This is a nightmare!" Morrow roared. "They've got complete control of that building, top to bottom. They've obviously got surface-to-air missiles, God only knows how many bad guys inside and now this bastard who wanted me to address him as God wants to speak to the President of the United States. Why the Space Museum?" The man was losing it but Bolan could forgive him his outrage and panic. "These bastards have blown up half the city."

Bolan checked the rooftop and spotted four armed figures crouched on the edge, overlooking Jefferson Street. Dead ahead, he saw the three big white vans parked in front of the Jefferson entrance, but across the street and against the grassy edge of the Mall. Bolan had some of the picture but knew enough. They were too close to a potential blast radius if the enemy got another wild hair.

"What else?" Brognola asked.

"Get all these vehicles back another fifty yards," Bolan said.

Morrow looked at Bolan. "Who are you?"

"He's with me and you'll take orders from him when necessary," Brognola said.

Bolan listened as Morrow gave Brognola the particulars on the communications setup.

"So, what are you waiting for?" Brognola asked the FBI agent.

"The vehicles, Agent Morrow," Bolan repeated.

The Fed grabbed his bullhorn. "Everybody, back up your vehicles! Give me fifty yards at least! Move it!"

"If I say hit the deck," Bolan told Morrow, "you make sure these men understand that."

The agent seemed to want to say something but nodded and passed on the word with another bellow through the horn.

Bolan watched as cops and Feds followed the order. The Executioner then took a moment to survey the Air and Space Museum. They could look at blueprints of the museum all they wanted, but Bolan knew there was no way to storm the place. It was primed to blow. Okay, he would wait until the enemy made contact with the President. It was demand time, put up or blow up.

The soldier was searching for an alternative way to get inside the building, have his own face-to-face with the enemy. He wasn't sure yet what he would do, much less say when he tracked down the terrorists but he knew of at least one demand he would issue, or else. Even still, he was forced to let them call the play in the next few minutes, take it from there.

Bolan only knew something had to be done, and fast. Already the city was a roving human time bomb of fear and anarchy. Looting and burning had already broken out across town. That was only a small part of the worst to come, he feared.

Morrow rolled his vehicle beside Bolan, craned his head out the window and said, "These assholes blew up half their own vehicles. How do they plan on getting out? Walk right up the street, blow us a kiss goodbye?''

Bolan just stared at Morrow as the FBI man punched in the number for the Oval Office.

''They don't plan on leaving here alive, you know that, don't you?'' Morrow said. ''We're on suicide watch here.''

12

According to the news, there had been twenty or more separate terrorist attacks, in and around the city. There were suicide car bombings at Reagan and Dulles airports, same thing on the Beltway. Three different bombings on the metro shut off the entire subway system to anyone other than the police and paramedics, who the media showed hauling out the body bags.

The horror show kept rolling, and Martika Kobeslav was forced to watch, a prisoner to some Apocalypse she never would have believed possible if she hadn't seen it with her own eyes. Shopping malls, awash in bodies, flames and debris of all kind, had turned into suburban battlegrounds. In Prince George County, a suicide bomber blew himself up as he bulldozed his truck through the emergency room doors of the local hospital. News choppers were hovering over the Potomac, reporting live on the mass exodus from Washington of anyone who owned a car, while looters pillaged and burned the city. News crews were on hand to bring the riots into the living room, up-close and personal, with the National Guard and D.C. police hosing down frenzied mobs with tear gas, rubber bullets and water bursting from fire hoses. The President of the United States was expected to come on national television and declare martial law but there was some delay, and the press secretary now fielded the flurry of questions hurled by clearly stunned and overwhelmed reporters in the President's absence.

It was madness but it didn't stop with the news.

Each time a reporter began listing casualty figures, she watched with fear and revulsion as the Arabs clapped each other on the back, embraced and congratulated one another in their native tongue.

To make it all the more sickening, Martika Kobeslav knew she might get nailed as a coconspirator in the deadliest, most massive terrorist attack ever launched against any country. And this wasn't Beirut or Tel Aviv, where car bombings and mad gunmen spraying crowds of innocents were standard sound bites for the newshounds.

Her world seemed primed to spin off its axis, cast her into an oblivion she suddenly craved to vanish into. If Kobeslav had known what she was getting into, she would have never taken the colonel's money. Her life meant more to her than anything. Oh, she would have weathered his threats, jerked him along with charm, a winning smile and nubile flesh, then disappeared into some country few people knew existed.

It was way too late now, she knew, for bitching and hand-wringing, and she was certainly far beyond the point of just walking away from it.

This, she thought, was indeed what they meant by the point of no return.

So, she was stuck in Senator Robert Spellman's home, forced to watch the Arabs bouncing with glee around the television. They scared her, but she wasn't about to show fear.

Yet they were only part of her anxiety. Both Senator and Mrs. Spellman were being held captive in their living room. The effects of the stun gun had worn off once they reached the senator's home. The Arabs had rolled right through the front doorway, taken down the hysterical Mrs. Spellman, but were forced to slap her around to stop the screaming. The Arab leader, Fazi, had ordered the phones torn out of the wall, the two Dobermans shot in the head and the place locked up tight. They were well off the beaten path, the split-level home surrounded by woods, the gravel driveway marked at the entrance with Private No Trespassing.

Spellman was now working on another vodka martini. For the past hour two of the Arabs took turns brooding over what looked like a radio backpack on the dining room table. They would stare at it, as if trying to will whoever they were waiting to hear from to call. There was some problem, Kobeslav was certain, and she sensed their mounting agitation the longer the radio stayed silent. The only plus she could see was they hadn't asked for her Makarov pistol, and she wasn't about to give it up now even if they did.

Again, she ignored the angry stare from Mrs.

Spellman as her husband moved to the wet bar. The Czech beauty crossed her long legs and caught the Arabs glancing at the skin she flashed. Mrs. Spellman scowled at the leg show.

For hours Kobeslav had seen the questioning looks Mrs. Spellman had thrown the senator. She suspected infidelity, smelled the truth as only a woman could, but she hadn't broached the subject. Other than the Arabs jumping for joy the silence was agonizing.

Kobeslav decided a drink for her nerves was in order, but she also needed a thrill fix. Something to fan the flames, create some excitement, get her mind off her problems.

"Relax, Mrs. Spellman," Kobeslav said, breaking the silence. "I have no further interest in your husband. I never did really, especially when he showed there's real meaning to the cliché about separating the men from the boys. Truth is, I've had teenage boys..."

"Silence!" Fazi roared, taking a step across the living room, his compact subgun coming up a few inches.

"Relax," Kobeslav told Fazi. "Just passing time. How about a drink, honey?"

She saw the senator as a worm now more than ever. He poured the drink on her command, as if keeping his hands busy or sucking down more booze would make it all go away. When he handed her a glass she returned his bitter scowl with a smile.

"Cheers," she said, lifting her glass. "To memories?"

"You bitch," he snarled. "Why? Is it money you people want?"

"Sit and shut your mouth!" Fazi shouted. "No, this isn't about money. We'll make no phone calls to the police to demand a ransom."

"Then what?" the senator whined. "What do you want?"

Fazi bared chipped teeth in a ghoulish smile. "This is about justice."

Mrs. Spellman hung her head and groaned in despair. "You're going to kill us, aren't you?"

"Not unless I receive orders to do so," Fazi said.

"So, who are you waiting to hear from, or do you intend to drag out the suspense?" Kobeslav demanded, and sipped her drink. "Are we supposed to be leaving here with those two, like they're luggage to carry around?"

"No more questions!" Fazi said. "No more talk."

There was an *or else* left out, she knew. Fair enough. Martika Kobeslav worked on her drink and lapsed into worried silence. She decided to kill time by coming up with a plan to get out of there and away from the crazy Arabs, then somehow flee the madness that had seized the entire city. It was only going to get worse if she stayed. Something told her that whomever they were waiting to hear from wasn't going to call in. They were either captured or dead or the kidnap scenario was just a ruse to draw police attention while the Arab's comrades fled the country.

Kobeslav was a survivor. She would keep the Makarov out of sight, keep the faith to herself. She hoped between their rejoicing and attention to the radio they had forgotten she was armed. When the time came, and their backs were turned, of course, she knew she could pump three quick bullets into their skulls. She had already killed one man, gotten past the nausea that came with the first kill. The next few should be easy, might even feed her craving for thrill like nothing else in life ever had. Three Arabs, bang, bang, bang. Move onto the Mrs. next, put her out of her marital hell. She'd save the senator for last.

When the opportunity showed, Kobeslav would quit this game and leave behind a few more bloody pieces of a puzzle for someone else to figure out. It was the least she owed herself for all her time, trouble and personal risk. She had money in the bank, after all, not to mention a little bit of the good life waiting to be salvaged.

Martika Kobeslav was her own woman and nobody's fool.

"MR. PRESIDENT, sir, I appreciate you moving so quickly to open a line of communication."

Colonel Becker had center stage near the Douglas DC-3 exhibit. He had the cellular phone in hand, Artillon and Biltman by his side, and dozens of hostages kneeling along the wall before him. Everyone was either looking at or to him, to either make it happen or go away.

They had set up a television set near the Golden Age of Flight gallery. The sound was now off, but Becker had been watching the screen for the past fifteen minutes waiting for the President to get online, hook the cops and Feds into the airwaves, no doubt, everyone wanting in on the act. The images of death and destruction that had flickered constantly across the screen told Becker all he needed to know. The opening phase of his war had been a total and astonishing success. Minutes ago, he had indulged in a moment of silence while he mentally tipped his hat to those who had given their lives for their cause. May God rest their warrior souls.

"Let's dispense with the preamble," Becker heard the President growl. "Who are you? And what do you want in order to release the hostages?"

"God, sir, you are talking to God, to answer your first question."

"You're insane! You're a killer of innocent men, women and children. If I call you anything I will refer to you as the devil."

"We're not getting off on the warm and fuzzy track I had hoped for, sir."

"Do you know how many Americans you and your horde have slaughtered? How many police officers you've killed who had wives and children who will never see them again?"

"As a soldier, sir, I can appreciate and regret their loss."

"Is that what you are? A soldier? You're an American?"

"Was, sir. Now I'm simply an instrument of the free enterprise system, I'm worldwide, doing what all good Americans do everyday. I go to work and I expect to get paid."

"This is about money?"

Becker ran a cold glance over his hostages, drawing inspiration from their terror. "I know this is an open line and you've got all your lackeys and Joint Chief bootlickers gathered." Becker heard someone call him a bastard in the background. "That's right, I'm a bastard, whoever said that. I'm a bastard the military trained to become the most efficient and ruthless killing machine in the world. I'm a bastard who died and resurrected himself and I'm here to show you what a few good men can do. You will either bow and scrape before me and bend to my will or I'll shove my wrath right down your throats using the blood of all those innocents you want to coddle so much. I hope you're reading me loud and fucking clear, gentlemen."

"Now it's vengeance? Which is it? Money or vengeance?"

"Both. Neither. Listen to me. You ever look around this country, sir, and see that's it all going to hell, that the animals own the streets. That decent men and women can't even walk down the sidewalk or drive their cars without feeling or being threatened."

"Skip the speech. You're hardly a crusader for law and order."

"That's where you're wrong. You can see on your television this very second just how thin the line is out there between law and order and anarchy. I've shown you just how weak America has become, just how ripe for the slaughter you are." Becker was savoring this moment in history and he wasn't about to give up the spotlight to anyone. "You know, there was a time, hundreds of years ago, of course, when a man controlled his own destiny, when his family honored and respected him as a man, as a provider and as a warrior. The Dark and the Middle Ages for example. The barbarian tribes, I'm referring to, and not just the Europeans. Yes, sir, there was a time when men rode up over the hill and looked the savages square in the eye. You know the deal? They were looking at their enemies who wanted to take everything they held dear. They would say to the would-be conquering savages, 'Hey, you want our women, you want our food? Is that right? Well, if you kill me, you can have it, because I won't live with the shame of having it taken from me.' How things have changed since then, but you know what they say about the more something changes. The power of the sword, sir, it still exists but in the hands of the most capable and most honorable of warriors. And I believe, sir, I've already won the hearts and minds of all concerned in your museum."

Becker had made his speech. He let the silence

go on, waiting for the President. "Sir, feel free to speak now."

"One last time. What do you want in order to release the hostages?"

"Ah, yes, the price tag for freedom, for their safe return to their crumbling society. Where spoiled and pampered professional athletes and rock stars make more money in one day than a school teacher, those people of honor who eke out an existence while shaping the minds and characters of the future."

"God damm it, I'm losing patience. Answer my question."

"Sir, this is a one-time, nonnegotiable deal. The going price for the safe return of everyone left alive and breathing around me is one billion dollars."

There was a pause on the other end. "What?"

"You heard me correctly."

"How do you expect me to come up with that kind of money?"

"You piss that much away in a little aid to some third world country nobody has ever heard of much less gives a damn about. Go to the bank, that's where you usually get money. Go to a bunch of banks. Print it, I don't care. I'll take old bills, new bills, twenties, fifties, hundreds, whatever, as long as they are real and unmarked. But don't attempt to pass off bogus paper or marked bills. Believe me, sir, I have experts on hand. And if any attempt is made to assault this complex..."

"I've been informed. You have the museum mined with plastic explosive."

"One billion dollars, sir. I want it delivered within twenty-four hours. That's your deadline, non-negotiable. I'm signing off. I suggest you and your peons get real busy. For every hour you go beyond my deadline, I will march five hostages out front and shoot them down, every hour on the hour."

Becker heard the angry voices in the background, the Cabinet members and the Joint Chiefs of staff brass clearly in an uproar.

"I'll be in touch, sir," Becker said and cut the connection.

He felt Artillon and Biltman watching him. He looked his two soldiers in the eyes. Their grim silence said it all. The demand was on the table, and the moment of truth was in the hands of the Oval Office. If they didn't open the bank Becker knew his team would go out in their own final blaze of glory. As it was deemed in the beginning, from the very day twelve dead men had signed on in blood.

Becker had just left them all with no choice. The game had taken on a whole new dimension. They were about to separate the men from the boys, the winners from the losers.

THE LINE had been checked by the Man's electronics experts before Hal Brognola put in the call. As far as they knew, Brognola could talk freely to the President.

Bolan waited while the big Fed went back and forth with the President, then finally laid it out to the Man.

The Executioner wanted inside the museum to lay out his own one-time offer. And Bolan wanted to be the bagman. There was no other way than to give Becker his billion. At least that was how the Executioner wanted it to appear. It was dicey, all around, and judging Brognola's tone and expression they were having a hard time selling it to the President.

The Crown Vic sat apart from the other official vehicles. The two men needed distance from any ears if they were to iron out the plan and keep Bolan's cover intact. Of course, the President was juggling dozens of official power players who wanted to run the show their way. Bolan knew the Man had cleared out the Oval Office and was currently speaking to Brognola free of advisors, political, military or otherwise.

But time was running out.

Bolan felt the tension rising in his belly. They needed this wrapped up, somehow, even if the Executioner was about to deliver a whole lot of promises he had no intention of keeping.

Bolan was putting together his plan, the sirens and flashing lights all around him constant reminders of anarchy, when he heard Brognola say, "Yes, sir. I understand. Yes, sir, I'll get back to you as soon as contact is made."

The Executioner had the job.

Brognola signed off and stared, long and hard, at the Executioner. "The Man laid down a couple of conditions, but he said to do it. First, let me raise this bastard, then we'll talk."

While Brognola punched in the numbers for enemy contact, Bolan took out both the .44 Magnum Desert Eagle and the Beretta 93-R and laid them on the roof of his rental.

"BECKER?"

He froze at the sound of his name coming over the cellular phone. The phone had rung a few seconds before, and he had answered, expecting the President.

They knew who they were dealing with, Becker thought. Maybe someone in the CIA had stepped up, or one of the terrorists had been captured. A police or FBI sketch artist would be going to work, comparing their faces with the photos in their ID jackets at Bragg...

It didn't matter.

"Who am I speaking to?"

"Brognola. Justice Department."

"I hope you bring me good news about my money."

"I want to send in a man to talk to you, Becker."

"There's nothing to discuss."

"There's plenty to talk about. You want your money, you talk to my man."

"I'm calling the shots, you don't tell me squat."

"Of course. Well?"

Becker suddenly had some questions of his own. There was only one logical course of action.

"Send him."

13

Bolan took the long walk up the steps. The soldier was grimly aware of one single and lonely fact, as he saw a gunman elbow a break in the wall of innocents and thrust open a door: it was all on his shoulders.

Whatever the Executioner did or didn't do, said or didn't say in the next few minutes would determine the fate of both the good and the bad, maybe an entire city. For Bolan this wasn't about glory, or muscling his way to the head of the table because he didn't believe anyone else worthy or good enough to get it done.

It was about saving lives. And he was there, on the front lines, running against the enemy clock. Indeed, time was quickly slipping away.

Bolan was no politician by any stretch, content to leave the word games and the power of persuasion over voters and campaign rivals to others. He was a soldier, first, last and always, living by the simple creed that actions speak louder than words. But over the hellish miles of his war against the cannibals he had learned the value of artful negotiating while role-playing. It had proved an invaluable tool, a form of deception, yes, but sometimes deceit and manipulation were the only ways to bring down an enemy that had the overwhelming edge in both men and firepower.

So he would become the negotiator, weighing the outcome for all concerned, but primarily going to bat for the innocents.

And the President had spoken with crystal clear intent. Condition one was that the enemy give them hostages in return for the first ransom delivery. If not, all bets were off and the museum was stormed, even at the risk of great loss of innocent life. Condition two would play itself out in the long run, if Bolan got it that far. And the President had passed on his expressed wish to Hal Brognola that he wanted the terrorists terminated with extreme prejudice at some juncture. The Man had wanted a plan of attack from Bolan and Brognola on his desk before midnight.

Bolan was about to go to work to at least lay the groundwork for what he had in mind.

"Welcome to your nightmare."

The Executioner paused at the door. He recognized the lean face, hawkish nose and icy blue eyes of Mark Freeman from the Fort Bragg jackets. Still smiling over his greeting, Freeman reached out and snatched Bolan inside the museum.

It didn't take a Ph.D. in psychiatry to feel the terror. It was a giant wave crashing over Bolan, complete with the harsh smells of sweat and fear, blood and bodily waste. Two more former Green

Berets—Paulsen and Baldwin, if he remembered correctly—dropped in beside the Executioner and marched him around the corner. In the distance, Bolan saw the radio, television and the dozen or so gunmen watching hostages near the Grumman G-21 Amphibian display. Ian Becker broke from the group, rolled up and stood, front and center, before Bolan. The ex-Special Forces Colonel looked a little worse for wear than the young man Bolan recalled from the jacket photo. But it was the same Becker, no doubt. Older, of course, but leaner and meaner, arrogance and anger alive and well in the eyes and set of his jaw.

Becker, his H&K MP-5 held low by his side, narrowed his gaze and studied Bolan. With his submachine gun Becker indicated for Bolan to raise his arms. He gave a nod past Bolan. As the soldier lifted his arms above his head, he felt two pairs of hands go through a rough frisking, head to toe.

Freeman reported, "Clean, sir."

Becker motioned that Bolan could drop his hands. "What's your name?"

"Belasko."

"What are you? FBI? CIA? Justice?"

"None of the above."

Suddenly Becker bared his teeth and nodded at his men. Before the soldier could react he was clubbed over the head with subgun butts and driven to his knees. Bolan rode out the pain, then Becker buried a boot into his gut. The wind gushed out Bolan's mouth, and he collapsed on his back as another blow across the head had him seeing more stars.

"Smart I can tolerate. Smart ass will get you killed."

Laid out, Bolan slowly sucked the air back into his starved lungs. He looked up through the haze and he found the muzzle of Becker's MP-5 in his face. Bolan didn't flinch, but only steeled his expression. It was part of the package deal, and Bolan had seen it many times before. The savage knew no other way than to inflict pain, wanting to break a man with his own fear, leave him vulnerable and begging for mercy.

"I asked you a question, Belasko."

"And I answered."

Something changed in Becker's eyes as the man loomed over Bolan. Maybe it was admiration, some fleeting respect that the Executioner had taken it to the edge and didn't crack.

"Well, how about this," Becker said, pulling back his subgun. "At least they sent me someone with a real pair. Get up."

Bolan took his time standing. He let the blood from the gash on top of his head run down the side of his face.

Becker nodded several times, squaring Bolan in the eye for a few heartbeats. "You're a soldier. A vet?"

"I was there."

"I can tell."

"Why?"

"I understand the question. Why? Consider this the Mount Everest for me and my men."

"Because it's there?"

"Sometimes the path chooses a man. Sometimes a man chooses the path. Some men make no choice at all."

Bolan held his ground. "And you?"

"The path chose me."

"You're telling me life left you no options?"

"You know who we are, then you know what happened."

"Consider me in the dark. Fill in the blanks."

Becker chuckled. "You know, Belasko I'm starting to kind of like you. You are one ballsy SOB. Hell, mister, I don't mind telling you, I'm looking at a soldier right now I would have given my left nut to have as part of my team."

"I'm not for sale or recruitment."

Becker ran another judging stare over Bolan. "How did you find out about us?"

"Biltman's SAVAK buddies."

"They put you on the scent. You hit that house, didn't you?"

"You've got one way to make it out of here."

"You mind answering the question first?"

"All right. I took five of your goons off the payroll."

Becker balked, assessing Bolan again, then chuckled. "Goddamn, I like you. A hitter, they send me a hitter who thinks he can drive one to the upper deck his last at bat of the season. I'm a baseball fan, you know that?"

"It wasn't part of the particulars in the jacket."

"Last decent thing about this country. Only thing I've really missed about it." A rueful shake of the head, then Becker went on. "Okay. So, you're the President's messenger service. You going to be the bagman for my cool billion?"

"That's not my call."

"No, it's mine. You just volunteered to get and to deliver my money."

"It's not that simple."

"I'm sure you overheard my little chat with the President."

"I did. But I have one nonnegotiable item myself."

"Which is?"

"I want a good-faith gesture."

"You want me to release some of these people."

"The children."

"The children? You're shitting me, right?"

"I usually say what I mean."

"Let me get this straight. You want me to just let you walk right out of here, kids following you out the door like some modern Pied Piper?"

"Yes."

"You understand what you're asking, soldier? All of a sudden I see a billion dollars walking off with the Pied Piper."

"Becker, I can tell you for a fact that if you don't give them something, you won't make it. Consider this. Let the children go, show them you've got a compassionate side.''

"That's a definite stretch in their eyes.''

"For appearance's sake, in your case.''

Becker laughed. "I'm listening.''

"If you let the children walk, you still have, what, five, six hundred hostages?''

"And while Delta Force or Navy SEALs are coming through my human walls, we start wasting hostages, blow the place clear into Virginia. How smart is that?''

"They're considering all options.''

"I'm sure they are,'' Becker said.

"No matter how many men you have here, you're stretching it thin to watch all these people. If this goes on much longer, how are you going to feed them? What about the basics, using the toilet?''

"This won't be some American Embassy situation in Tehran. And if they come at us, it will be Desert Storm but on an apocalyptic scale. Uncle Sam starts sacrificing his own, the masses across the country may come unglued. I'm talking armed rebellion by civilians. Lot of people watch those spooky shows where their government is lying to them about everything from UFOs to JFK.''

"I understand. You're making a statement about how you see America. We've become the new Roman Empire to you.''

"You're goddamn right I'm making a statement! Watch the riots right now on TV. Case closed. That's just some of it.''

"How long do you think you can keep those hostages standing at the doors before they drop from exhaustion, maybe make a break for it? People kneeling, edged out by terror, jump and blindside one of your own?"

"I'll work out the details. Hey, I know how it looks, but I'm not here to see people suffer."

Bolan choked down the grim chuckle. "The children."

"And if I don't?"

"Then you don't."

Becker worked his jaw, but Bolan sensed the man considering his options. "Biltman!"

"Sir?"

"I need a minute with you."

Bolan saw Daniel Biltman march out of the shadows near the Jet Aviation hall. Becker wheeled, met Biltman and led him toward the low wall in front of the Grumman G-21 Amphibian.

Bolan glanced over his shoulder at Freeman; Becker's man greeting him with an arrogant smile. The Executioner felt the tension coil in his gut. The hand was played, and the enemy had all the right cards at the moment. Whatever decision Becker made would determine where it went from there.

Waiting, Bolan searched the faces of the hostages. He saw terrified mothers hugging small children, stroking their heads, whispering into the ears of those children who quietly sobbed. Fathers, also scared for their families, a few of them clearly seething in impotent rage. It was all Bolan could do to hold back his own rage over the madness inflicted on the innocent. These were families who before now had normal lives. They raised children, went to work, paid bills and wanted a better life for their young. They were something Becker clearly loathed, maybe something either Becker never had or wanted, Bolan thought. He certainly didn't care about it, clearly held these hostages in contempt, viewing them as weak, expendable in his quest to be God, as he wanted to be addressed. That was just the nature of Becker's beast.

Gradually, as the minutes passed, Bolan could feel the hope and the promise breaking through the fear. They were good people, he could see it, feel it, and they wanted nothing more than to see their children spared. A small comfort indeed, but Bolan was taking the right gamble.

They could never understand, of course, the face of evil the Executioner had seen. It could go either way, but for damn sure it was only going to get uglier. Whatever happened here their lives had been changed forever, make no mistake.

Bolan saw Becker heading his way. At first read, the Executioner feared the worst. The colonel stopped in front of Bolan. The silence dragged. The soldier held Becker's cold stare, waiting to hear words he dreaded.

"Why don't you give us a hand rounding up the kids, Belasko."

THERE WAS a sick punch line coming, but Bolan pushed aside thoughts of doom. It was eating up more time than Becker liked, his men snarling and barking for the children to get moving. Soon after threats were issued all around and parents were forced to accept the circumstances, the children were rounded up and ordered out the Jefferson Street doors. Bolan supervised, gently pulling a few of the smaller children away from sobbing mothers, offering words of comfort where he could.

"Don't let them hurt my baby. She's all I've got."

Bolan accepted the toddler from the woman and assured her, "Your baby will be fine. You have my promise."

The soldier carried the infant in his arms toward the Jefferson lobby. On the Mall several MedStar choppers were descending beyond the line of official vehicles. Becker had already put the word to Brognola as soon as the roundup began. Ambulances were now swinging into view, paramedics disembarking, ready to receive the children. Some of the children ran, some walked and stumbled, the faltering ones clearly more exhausted from the ordeal. The children who lagged behind were taken in by D.C. police daring to cross the no-man's-land of Jefferson.

Bolan looked at a teenaged boy moving in front of him and asked, "Son?" The soldier could see Becker on the way, and Bolan wanted his hands free, just in case. "Will you?"

The boy nodded, and took the infant from Bolan.

"That was real touching."

There was new menace in Becker as Bolan waited until the ex-Special Forces leader marched up to him.

"You're thinking this was too easy, Belasko. Maybe I caved, I'm weak. Here it is. If I don't get my money, if me and my men don't walk away, I'll bring this entire city down. Why did I just hand the children over to you, you ask? Relay this to your President. I have three, count them, three nuclear devices armed and ready to go. You think I'm bluffing, call me on it."

The punch line. But Bolan had already suspected Becker had his way out already calculated.

Becker produced a slip of paper and handed it to Bolan. "That's the address of a gym in Maryland. That's a locker number there, too. I suggest you take some HAZMAT boys along. Whatever you do, don't drop what you find, especially if there's a nice wind blowing toward town."

"What else, Becker? You want a parade, an escort out of here?"

Becker gave Bolan a cold laugh. "In other words you're asking me how I plan on walking. We're not walking, soldier. We're not driving. We're going to fly out of here." Becker paused, letting that sink in. "And you know what? Since I've grown so fond of you, you're going to help us."

Bolan just stared a moment into the face of evil, then turned and walked. There was nothing left to say. There was only a new horror to try to fathom, and hopefully defend against.

He had won a major coup perhaps, getting the children freed. But the Executioner now knew their problems had just mounted to the point where Becker could very well pull it off.

The stakes had just gone nuclear, or worse, depending on what was found in the gym locker.

Bolan waited until the last of the children were out the door. Then the Executioner stepped outside into what was now more than ever a very uncertain twenty-something hours, and counting.

14

A joint FBI and Justice Department special task force had secured the gym's perimeter. They had ordered all civilians inside to clear out or face detainment. That came straight from the Oval Office—seize the building, cordon off the area for six blocks around the compass. With full-scale evacuation handled by the National Guard, an Army HAZMAT team had rolled in wearing contamination suits, then used bolt cutters to open the locker in question. They found one vial of a clear substance, which was flown to Quantico, and analyzed within the hour by the FBI. The substance was anthrax.

Bolan had gotten that latest batch of grim news through Brognola.

It had been a tense briefing in the big Fed's office while Brognola laid out what Bolan already knew about anthrax. The big Fed was running on fear, even more so now in light of what they both now knew. Anthrax could be easily dispersed, a few grams from a rooftop and thousands would start dying. Catch a decent wind and anthrax could be blown over half the city, one sprawling lethal sneeze. It would take three days before the first victim hit the ground, sweating and shaking, appearing to be struck down by nothing more than the flu. But once it started it wouldn't stop. It was a contagion, spread through the air or by simple human contact.

Doomsday for the United States of America was on the horizon.

Anthrax, Bolan knew, could be purchased on the black market, almost as easy as buying a few kilos of cocaine if the money was right. The Russian Mafia, Iraq—despite all United Nations-CIA efforts to root out and shut down Hussein's chemical and germ warfare-producing plants—and the North Koreans were all in the game of selling mass death through germ agents. There was even a rumor the Colombian drug cartels were interested in anthrax. A few spores was all it would take to begin manufacturing this horror.

Faced with capture, the Executioner knew the terrorists holding the museum hostage would use anthrax as a last ditch gasp. It certainly compounded the nightmare scenario. Where Becker had gotten his hands on anthrax and how he had smuggled it into America, well, Bolan would leave those unanswered questions to the military and intelligence communities. He had work to do.

To make matters even more grim, the soldier had the dubious distinction of telling the President Washington D.C. was the potential ground zero for a nuclear strike. The President had been urged to leave the White House for Camp David but he wouldn't hear of it. And the President could only hold back from his Cabinet and the Joint Chiefs the double-billed threat of nuclear-chemical blackmail for a few more hours. Of course, the media wouldn't get a clue, not the first leak, the President had said, or the panic would spread beyond the city, martial law maybe declared across the country.

That was sixty-eight minutes ago, according to Bolan's watch. The Executioner and Brognola had hashed it over, A to Z, then dumped their plan over to the President, who was currently exercising executive privilege and getting together the money.

Bolan wasn't about to stand and watch the clock.

The office was in the basement of the Justice Department. It was spartan, only a couch, chair and desk, but it was quiet and secluded.

The Executioner manhandled Khalif Mustapha through the door by the scruff of the neck, then sent the Syrian on a nose-first dive into the desk. Brognola stepped in behind Bolan and shut the door.

"I need some straight answers," the Executioner told Mustapha who hauled himself to his feet, watching Bolan with fear. Bolan dumped the manila envelope on the desk. "Open it."

Mustapha did. "I'm supposed to know these men?"

"Take a good look. What you say next may determine whether you walk or spend twenty years behind bars."

"For what?"

Brognola stepped up beside Mustapha. "For aiding and abetting terrorists, for starters."

"Is that some new law that was just passed?"

"It's called conspiracy," Brognola said.

"Who are these terrorists I'm supposed to know? These men here look American."

"Look at the pictures," Bolan growled. "All of them."

They waited while Mustapha went through the pile. He stopped abruptly. "Do you have a pen? A felt one."

Brognola walked around the desk and opened the drawer. Fishing, he produced a pen for Mustapha. Bolan looked over the Syrian's shoulder as he uncapped the pen. It was the one photo of Sampson, the Butcher, the CIA had been able to produce. Mustapha painted a mustache on the cadaverous face, then scribbled shoulder-length hair on the sides.

"Yes. That's him. He thought he could fool someone with the wig and mustache."

"We're listening," Bolan prodded.

"He came to me a little over six months back. He needed a house in Vienna. He gave me cash to help him find one. Said it was urgent. He needed one with a garage, he was very specific about the garage."

"He knew about your problem," Bolan said.

"What problem?"

"The problem with your brother and cousin. Go on. Did you land him a house?"

"Yes, but not through Hastings Realty."

"Do you have an address?" Bolan asked.

"No, but I know where to get one."

BOLAN AND BROGNOLA were alone in the Justice man's office. Using the red line to the Oval Office, Brognola had his ear to the phone. The Executioner waited, listening to a one-sided conversation between the President and the big Fed.

"Yes, sir. I understand. Yes, sir. I'll pass that on to Striker."

Brognola hung up. Bolan met the big Fed's grim stare.

"Two hundred million, Striker. It will be in two diplomatic pouches. I'm having agents pick it up now. The President said to run with your plan. The two hundred mil is the first delivery. More hostages will have to be released if Becker wants a second round of cash. Tell him that's nonnegotiable. The plan is dicey, but you heard me sell it to the President. If it doesn't work the Man will have no option but to launch a surgical strike against the museum. He's weighed the potential loss of life across the entire area, with the use of the nukes and anthrax against the hostages."

"Becker will blow the place before the first troops hit the doors."

"He's not talking about going through the front doors."

Bolan stared hard at Brognola as the realization of what was on the table sank in. "An air strike?"

Brognola nodded. "Kurtzman tracked down that address for us. I assume you're going to take a ride to Vienna?"

SAMPSON WAS restless. He had seen enough news reports to know their plan was succeeding, so far. But with the media kept well back from the museum and in the dark about what was really going on inside, Sampson feared any number of problems could arise. He didn't like lack of information, especially not in his business.

He checked his watch. He only hoped the President would deliver the billion dollars on time before the jets landed on the Mall. If not, they would be grounded, his handpicked pilots from the Air America days nervous to get airborne and see some more money.

The Butcher went to the window and slipped the curtain back a few inches. It was a quiet suburb, nestled in the heart of Vienna. Lights were on in the split levels across the street. An hour before he had seen a police car cruise slowly past. He wondered what that was about.

Paranoia came with the turf. He wasn't about to see his hopes and dreams come crashing down now.

Three decades of planning and shelling out cash made from the sale of drugs and guns to land the ordnance, buy up and train an army of Muslim fanatics. So far it had gone so easily it was almost frightening.

Stay focused, he told himself, it was almost over. But why did he feel as if he was being watched?

The money, think about all that cash. It was about the money, of course, but it was also an in-your-face statement from all of them to the powers that be in

America. Years before, Sampson had seen the decline of America coming and planned accordingly to salvage the golden years of the future. It was easy enough to walk away from the CIA, maybe doing a contract hit or two over the years, just to keep some crucial contacts close. But still there were a few spooks around who had known all along Sampson and his Phantom Alpha Six were alive and in the game of drug and gunrunning. It was a detail he had never bothered to go into at length with Becker.

Sampson checked the yard. What was that? He searched the hedges near the garage. Did he just see a shadow over that way? Something moved. Sampson was reaching for the holstered Glock when the something materialized—a shaggy dog. The dog sniffed around the lawn, then scampered off.

Sampson laughed. Pull it together. He needed a beer.

He reached for the doorknob, checking that the alarm system was activated. It was, but it was a habit he couldn't break.

The man known as the Butcher was opening the door, imagining the first taste of cold beer on his tongue, when he discovered his paranoia had not gotten the better of him.

Sampson froze as the sound-suppressed muzzle was stuck under his chin. He caught a glimpse of the ice blue eyes on the business end of that piece before he was shoved back into the living room and relieved of his weapon.

"I UNDERSTAND they call you the Butcher."

Bolan had taken a chair from the dining room and positioned it six feet from the gray-skinned skeletal figure. Sampson showed the Executioner a smile as he clasped his hands in his lap. He was a picture of calm and cool, sitting in the leather recliner, holding Bolan's stare.

"Where are the ADMs?"

"The what?"

Bolan lifted the Beretta 93-R and shot the Butcher in the shoulder. The man yelped, clutched the bloody hole, then gritted his teeth and cursed Bolan.

"You cut people," the Executioner said. "I can shoot you up. Little by little. Make it last all night. Only I have to get back to the museum and take some money to your buddy, Becker."

Sampson pulled it together, seeming to absorb the pain through his eyes. "You mind if I have a smoke?"

"If it will loosen your tongue."

The ghoul fired up a cigarette. "Okay, but I have one condition."

"I'm not here to hand you a deal."

"No, you're here to deal me out. I talk, you make it quick."

"Given your track record, that's more than you deserve."

"Well?"

Bolan nodded. "Okay. My question now?"

"Hell, you'd search the house anyway. They're in the garage."

"All three?"

"Two. I don't know where the third one is."

Bolan placed his aim between Sampson's legs.

"I don't! I'm telling you the truth!"

"No need to shout. Where do you think it is?"

Sampson inhaled on his cigarette. "Only Becker and a few of his people know. He wouldn't tell me. I guess that was his one way to make sure I lived up to my end."

"Which is?"

"Getting the planes there."

"When do they fly?"

"Anytime. I send out one signal by pager to the pilots. Another to Becker to let him know they're on the way."

"And the anthrax?"

Sampson balked. "I got that about a year ago. North Koreans. The vial in the gym locker?"

"It's been taken care of already."

"That was all there was. Bastard North Koreans got nervous dealing with me."

"I wonder why? Maybe they saw the same play coming you gave your KGB pals."

"Whatever. That vial was just supposed to put some more heat on you people to speed getting the money."

"There's something else you want to tell me. I can smell it. Don't hold back now."

Sampson blew twin funnels of smoke out his nose. "Two aces in the hole. Senators Walker and

Spellman. They were snatched. They're being held in their respective homes. Families also.''

"To make sure Becker has a safe flight."

Sampson nodded. Bolan listened as the ghoul laid out the particulars on the kidnappings. Another plan of attack took shape for Bolan. He had his work cut out.

"Some of the terrorists, I'm sure they're walking around, waiting to hear from you."

"The ones who didn't blow themselves up were to link up in Warrenton. They were to wait for me to contact them."

"I'll need directions." Bolan spotted the cellular phone on the coffee table, stood, picked it up and dumped it in Sampson's lap. "First call and tell them you're on the way."

Bolan waited while the Butcher put the call through. When Sampson finished delivering the message, he signed off and asked, "How did you find me?"

"Mustapha took your money."

"That bastard." Sampson shook his head, ground out his smoke and lit another cigarette. Bolan asked for the directions to the terrorist safe house again and Sampson gave it to him in fine detail.

"Go ahead and send the signal to your flyboys and Becker."

Bolan leveled the Beretta at a point right between Sampson's eyes as the Butcher reached into his pants pocket. The Executioner watched as Sampson worked the buttons on what looked like a high-tech pager, sure to have long distance capability.

"All done. It's a little early, the colonel may get nervous."

"He's already nervous."

"I'm sure," Sampson said. "Anything else?"

"Not that I can think of."

"Can I finish my smoke?"

"A couple more puffs."

"You know, it's funny," Sampson said, chuckling. "All I kept thinking about before you showed up was a cold beer. One lousy cold beer, that's all I wanted. Guess that's the least of my problems now, huh?"

"I don't think you'll get a cold one in hell."

Sampson ground out his smoke. "I don't think so either. End of discussion?"

The Executioner proved to the Butcher he was a man of his word and put one right between his eyes.

15

The Butcher's directions were on the money.

On a call back to Brognola en route, Bolan had told the big Fed the score. Two ADMs were now down, the Justice Department at that very moment on-site with one dead renegade CIA agent to greet them. The soldier had found them in the garage. The Russian version of the U.S. Special Forces backpack nuke was a crude replica at first glance, but Bolan didn't give it a thorough inspection or wait around for the cleanup crew to arrive.

It was going to be a busy night.

The two-story farmhouse was planted out in the middle of the country. The Executioner had found a dirt road that ran parallel to the target house. With nothing but the moon and the stars to guide him, the soldier had moved in on foot. Through his infrared binoculars, he watched two sentries near the front porch, smoking and talking. Submachine guns were slung over their shoulders. Seeing that the motor pool consisted of three luxury vehicles, the warrior figured twelve to fifteen of Becker's boys had to be taken care of.

There was no time to waste. Bolan needed this

foray wrapped, quickly and cleanly. He'd brought enough to this party to get the job done.

He shadowed beyond the brush, careful not to make any noise until he positioned himself fifty yards out from the east side of the farmhouse. He slipped the M-16/M-203 combo off his shoulder. A light burned beyond the side window, marking the Executioner's bull's-eye. He saw shadows moving around behind the curtain. From the satchel he took a 40 mm flash-stun grenade and loaded it into the M-203's breech.

The Executioner was ready.

An argument appeared to break out on the front stoop between the two sentries. He caught a couple of names: Abi and Kamil. He gave it brief and angry reflection, wondering how many innocent lives those two had snuffed, how many ruined families they had left behind to mourn the dead, to somehow pick up the pieces and try to get on with it.

These bastards were in for a taste of their own poison, and Bolan wanted to see them burned down in the worst way.

Another figure emerged from the front doorway and got into it with his terrorist brethren. Bolan figured the closest neighbor in the vicinity was a good half mile away. He was going to make some noise but he would be gone before the first neighbor was roused by all the sound and fury.

The Executioner took aim.

The trio quit arguing and then gave the field

stretching away from the front of the house a long search before vanishing into the living room.

The Executioner fired.

It streaked true.

Bull's-eye.

The calling card that would leave them senseless and reeling smashed through the window. On the run, and even at a distance, Bolan closed his eyes against the blinding flash. It would take them at least several seconds of wondering what the hell was happening to get it together.

The Executioner hit the motor pool, stopping near the front stoop, thirty yards out. Voices, shouting in panic, flayed the night.

The Executioner was ready and waiting when the first three terrorists came staggering out of the smoke cloud. He held down the trigger of the assault rifle, locked onto full auto, as they stumbled across the stoop. Weapons in the hands of blind men were firing everywhere, stuttering off a few rounds even as they were greeted by a maelstrom of 5.56 mm death. A few men came at Bolan, coughing and cursing, but they were chopped down by the soldier's sweeping burst of autofire and sent screaming back across the porch.

The Executioner wasn't taking any chances. He counted seven bodies stretched across the porch, but heard some hacking inside the house. A few rats still scurried about in the nest.

Bolan loaded the M-203 with a 40 mm grenade. He fired the first bomb straight through the front doorway. It was going off, blowing out the front face of the house in a clap of thunder and billowing fire, when another 40 mm round was dumped in on top of it.

One more for good measure and the Executioner brought the house down.

The farmhouse was reduced to kindling, and fire breathed to life in a sudden hungry whoosh. Bolan was moving off when he spotted a figure blast out of a heap of rubble on the west end. A bloody mess came screaming from the flames, sweeping the subgun.

Bolan emptied his clip into the hardman and flung him back into the fire. With a fresh magazine slapped home, he gave it another few stretched seconds, waiting for anymore terrorists who might have gotten lucky enough to weather the storm.

No takers.

He moved off and gave the back end of the house a search. No one.

The fire roared, a voracious force strobing the dark as if the lights of a football stadium had just been snapped on. If there were any wounded left in that inferno they were human toast.

It was a done deal, at least here.

"JUST LIKE an early Christmas, Colonel. I'd say the bank of America has been declared open, sir."

Bolan watched as Becker and Vinyard rifled through the diplomatic pouches. Becker shot the sergeant a frown.

"Don't get too happy." A few of the Arabs were standing, looking over Becker's shoulder. He felt the need to address them. "Yeah, it's payday. If you're assuming everyone gets a fair cut, you're right. Now go man your posts."

"May I have a word with you, in private," one of the Arabs asked.

"When we're in the air, we'll talk all you want. That good enough for you?"

The Arabs didn't appear convinced everything was beautiful but marched off to guard the hostages.

Bolan waited while stacks of bills were hauled out, examined by a few of Becker's troops. They were snapped, held up to flashlights, flipped around before bills were chosen at random and put under a scope that looked to Bolan like an infrared beam.

"They're real, Becker," Bolan said.

"I've got a mixed bag here. Hundreds, twenties, fifties. Lots of new bills. Too many new bills," Becker stated.

They had the night lights on. Quiet as a tomb, the museum had an eerie soft glow. Shadowed faces of hostages stared out at the flurry of activity.

Becker stepped up to Bolan. "That's only two hundred million. I've got five electronic counters. It'll take some time to make sure it's real and all there. Hey, not that I don't trust you, Belasko, but it will give me some peace of mind to know things are running smooth. My problem is the generator's starting to run low. Meaning time is running out fast.

You want to tell me why my bullshit antenna is up?''

"The kind of money you want takes time to come up with. They're printing the bulk of it."

"Print faster. Better yet, open every fucking bank in Maryland and Virginia and clean them out. I want to see some old bills next time."

"What are you worried about? I'm sure you've got a few cleaners on the other end."

"Or maybe I've got an island in the South Pacific all to myself, and I'll bury it in the sand. Don't start inquiring about my business. We clear?''

"Crystal."

"I've got another problem, friend. My pilots are on the way. In two hours they'll be on the Mall. They may get nervous if they have to sit out there too long."

"We can take this out of here. Finish the transaction in a place of your choosing."

Bolan waited while Becker considered it. Unless he was landing a C-130 on the Mall he wouldn't be able to take all the hostages along with his own people. But Bolan had planted the idea to wrap up the money deal elsewhere, and he needed it sold before he walked out again. It was the only way the Executioner could bring down the hammer on Becker and his savages.

"Right," Becker grunted. "As soon as we're airborne the President has a few F-16s up our asses and blow us out of the sky."

"I understand you have radar. You see anything on your screen?"

"Not yet, no."

"The President is willing to pay you. Give us something in return. Give up the hostages, give the building back and I'll personally deliver the rest of the money. And why would you worry now about some F-16s? You've got the edge."

"That's right. Three aces. I can set them off anywhere, anytime. Not only that," Becker said and proceeded to tell Bolan about the kidnapped senators. "It gets better, huh. For me, that is."

"Sounds like you've got it all figured out."

"Just remember that."

"Try to work with me here, Becker. I can maybe deliver another two hundred, but getting the rest together is going to eat a good part of the day."

Becker paused. "Okay. I'll work with you. I'll be talking to Brognola in a few minutes. Make sure I've got my landing strip under control. Two hours, Belasko. I want another two hundred million. Do that, me and my men walk out of here with the hostages. We board, give you back these people and fly on. I know you've got eyes in the sky, AWACS, Hawkeyes, whatever, that are going to keep track of us. I can live with that. When we're clear of Washington airspace I'll give you further instructions. For each time I feel even the least bit threatened or my bullshit radar is lit up like the Fourth of July, I'll set off an ADM. I so much as see a flock of geese or a UFO cross my path I'll get real nervous. You got my package in the locker, I assume?''

"Yes."

"So, you know it gets even better from where I stand."

"Well, I guess I'd better go round up some more money."

"Damn straight. You're dismissed."

Bolan turned and walked away. It was better than the soldier had hoped for, but he had counted on fraying nerves and greed on their part all along. Becker didn't know it yet, but he'd just swallowed the bait. The rest was up to Bolan, and he intended to deliver.

THEY WERE ahead of schedule, and that bothered Becker. While the money machines rolled the colonel stepped toward the Jefferson lobby. No, something didn't feel right at all.

First, Sampson had paged him too early for comfort. He couldn't radio the Butcher, aware that no matter how secure he believed the line, they could break in and trace the call. He couldn't afford to lose those ADMs. The anthrax was a smoke screen, of course, but the Americans didn't know that. He held all the right cards, yet something was missing, something he was overlooking. But what?

Second, the Arabs kept glaring at him and his men. They looked touchy, worried. A lot of money was at stake and he could almost read their thoughts, seeing the greed through their eyes. When they were airborne he would have to hand out all manner of promises to the Arabs. No sweat. Promises were made to be broken.

So far things were shaping up. Belasko was a soldier's soldier, a straight-shooter, or so Becker wanted to believe. He would get the money. Then how come he had this nagging ball in his gut?

Heat. It had been unseasonably hot, even beyond the first week officially ending the summer. They'd caught a few cool days here and there, but the weather changed almost daily. Weird. And wrong.

Becker strode toward a group of hostages. "Who lives here?" Scared, confused faces stared back and the colonel was forced to raise his voice, snarling, "I'm not going to hurt the person who answers me." He repeated his question and a man raised his hand. "What kind of summer did you have?"

"It was…hot. Extremely hot."

"What about rain?"

"They said it was one of the driest summers on record."

"When was the last time there was rain? Speak up!"

"I don't know."

"It's been that long, is that what you're saying."

Becker heard the man confirm his fear. He raised Weathers on the handheld radio. "How far down did you go?"

"Sir?"

"How far beneath the surface?"

"I'd have to say, five, six feet, sir."

Becker bit down the curse. "But you're not sure?"

"No, sir, it was dark."

"Damn it. Could it have been two feet?"

"It could have been ten, I didn't look up."

"But it could have been lower than ten?"

"I can't say for certain, sir. We were in kind of a hurry. Can I ask, sir, is there a problem?"

"I hope not. Man your station. Our birds are on the way. Let me know if anything looks unusual out there."

"Affirmative, sir."

Becker signed off and began to pace. If the tide fell any lower due to lack of rain, if they spotted it, if there was some problem on Sampson's end...

"Sir, is there some problem?"

Becker turned toward Vinyard, "I hope not, Sergeant."

"It looks like the money is there, sir. And it's real. Sir, can I feel free to speak?"

"I'm listening."

"Two hundred million, Colonel, that's a lot of money. Our pilots are on the way."

Becker had heard enough. "I understand where you're headed with this, Sergeant. The answer is no." He lowered his voice, saw a few too many of the Arabs glaring at him. "I, we, haven't come this far to take some chump change. You see our Arab comrades, the way they're looking at us. Divide that amount between what, eighty or so men? And our Butcher pal is getting ten percent off the top?"

"I understand, sir, but..."

"Save it. Raise those pilots now and get me an ETA. Move out, Sergeant."

Becker felt all eyes watching him. He stood, alone. He caught a sudden whiff of fear, and wondered if the smell came off himself.

BOLAN MADE the second delivery a little less than two hours later.

As he walked back out the Jefferson doors he could still feel the enemy's taut nerves. Becker hadn't said a word during the drop. The man sensed he had some problems. It was heating up. So be it. All Bolan wanted was to get the enemy out of the museum and in the air.

The soldier was crossing the street, heading for Brognola when the first of three aircraft began to lower over the museum. As Becker had ordered, all squad cars and ambulances were lined up at the edge, giving Becker his landing strip. To help guide the pilots in, the colonel had ordered every light that could flash to stay on.

Bolan watched the first of the jets touch down, kicking up a funnel of dust as it taxied past.

Brognola's grim expression was clearly outlined in the strobing lights. "You know what those are?"

The soldier did. "Gulfstreams. C-20s."

"Right. The military version. VIP transport. Now you want to tell me where the hell Becker got those?"

"A housecleaning on our end will have to wait."

"Well, at least we know they won't be taking the hostages. Even if they're stripped down you can't squeeze, what, more than twenty-five passengers in each?"

"Roughly twenty, including crew."

"Striker, I just got word from the Stony Man Farm. The last pouch is on the way and will be in my office in sixty minutes."

"I hear good news for a change."

"Cowboy Kissinger came through," Brognola said, referring to Stony Man's chief armorer and weapons expert. "We need to touch base with the President one more time. It's all touch-and-go, Striker. Everyone is chomping at the bit, burning up the Man's ear. If we don't make it happen in the next few hours..."

"I understand."

And Bolan did. The problem was the one ADM still out there.

"The President has assured me these aircraft won't be fired upon. He's using up a lot of favors, Striker. I can appreciate what he's going through. Political fallout is the least of his worries."

"You can tell him failure was never an option."

The radio crackled in Bolan's rental car. Becker's voice came on. "Brognola, Belasko. Pick up."

The big Fed did the honors. "Brognola here."

"We're coming out."

16

The hostages were released in waves. Bolan figured it was Becker's order how they split up on Jefferson. There were so many hostages streaming through the doors, Bolan couldn't even venture a head count. Not that it mattered. It was good enough they were being released, marching by the law and the paramedics out of harm's way to freedom.

One wave of newly freed captives headed east, the other half west. Some ran, some walked. A few stumbled and fell, then were gathered up by family, friends or fellow ex-hostages. Special Agent Morrow informed Brognola hostages were running out the front doors on the Independence side, and Brognola told the FBI man to relay the order to get personnel over there on the double. Becker certainly liked his confusion and chaos, Bolan knew.

The calls had already been put in to all available medical and Army personnel. The D.C. police, acting under FBI orders via Brognola, moved as close to the edge of the Mall as possible, directing the hostages to the waiting ambulances and med stations that were set up.

Bolan suspected Becker was saving himself a human wall. The ex-Special Forces leader didn't disappoint.

They came out, submachine guns in full display while at least five hardmen showed RPG-7s. The terrorist army kept the hostages in front of them as captive and captor alike made the long, slow walk down the steps. Not taking any chances, now that he figured the rest of his payday was in sight, Becker had the human shield rolled down his flanks. Twenty Arabs backpedaled, picking up the rear with more hostages at gunpoint, Becker and company moving the whole wall of terror ahead, step by tense step.

Then a conflict broke out among the police ranks. Bolan caught some of it, then the voices were clearly raised in angry protest.

"You just going to let these murdering bastards take the money and fly off? You know how many cops have died here because of them?"

Becker caught the trouble, too. "Belasko? What the hell's going on over there? You get those cops under control this second. I see one gun pointed this way, I start killing people. I'll blow this fucking museum, I'll blow those three vans in your face."

"Take it easy, Becker!" Bolan shouted.

"Fuck that! Get it together, Belasko. You've got five seconds. I've got my thumb on the button."

Bolan saw three uniformed policemen break rank and file. Agent Morrow was grabbing one of them by the shoulder.

Brognola marched off in that direction. "You! What's your name, officer?"

"Carlton." He answered as he wrenched free of Morrow. "You must be this Justice hotshot forking over a billion dollars to these assholes. I've got wives and kids who want to know why their husbands and fathers won't be coming home tonight. You want to tell me how I should go about telling them the Justice Department pays terrorists to kill cops?"

"Fall back, officer, right this second. Or I'll have you relieved of your weapon and detained."

They didn't budge. Carlton said, "I want an answer!"

"The simple answer, Officer Carlton," Brognola said, "is there isn't one."

"Captain Carlton!"

"Captain Carlton. I'm sorry for your losses—our losses. This thing isn't over." Brognola held his ground. "We've got scared hostages to tend to, maybe some of them in shock. Now, do you want to blow this thing up so that a lot more innocent people die, or do you want to give your fellow officers a hand in helping the people being released? I need an answer, Captain."

Bolan could well appreciate the cop's rage. To the men in blue, the FBI, perhaps even to an entire nation right then, it certainly appeared as if the President had his will bent by the enemy's demands. At the moment the home team looked weak.

If they only knew, Bolan thought.

Carlton cursed, then told his officers to fall back. Brognola issued an order to Morrow. "First man I see draw a weapon without my order will be fired and arrested on the spot, then punished severely. That's straight from the President. Pass that on.''

Brognola headed back and Becker called out, ''Hey, Belasko! You've got that excitement squared away!''

''Keep moving, Becker!''

They did. The C-20s slowly taxied up the Mall and parked behind Bolan. The turbo fan engines blew up dust and grit as they revved.

The human wall was marched past Bolan. Becker grabbed one hostage, his MP-5 draped across the woman's chest, and broke from the pack. ''Keep them moving, Vinyard!''

Bolan stared into the eyes of evil, waiting for Becker to speak.

Becker threw a piece of paper on the ground and looked set to laugh. ''Here's a map and, in case you get lost, the radio frequency you can use to reach us. You've got until noon today. Remember. I've got the power. See you later.''

Bolan watched, a cold ball of anger coiling in his belly. He saw the hostages then released, shoved away as the terrorists began boarding the three military jets.

''Let's get back to my office,'' Brognola said.

Bolan hesitated as he watched the cabin doors shut. The C-20s began the taxi east. At the end of the Mall, the first jet wheeled and began the long run, turbo engines shrieking as it streaked back. The Executioner picked up the paper and moved toward his vehicle. The first jet blew past just as the soldier took the wheel of his Crown Vic.

Then the first of the three military jets seemed to fly straight at the Washington Monument, as if it was on a suicide run, then the wing dipped to port.

Bolan raced across the Mall, watching the night swallow the enemy. They were gone, but not forgotten.

THE LAST POUCH was bottom-heavy by seventy-five pounds. Bolan hefted it. It would be the last one delivered. The extra weight would be the first tip-off maybe, but further examination—after they hopefully took the money out for a count as they had been doing so far—would reveal the message painted at the bottom. Bolan stared into the diplomatic pouch. The artist in question was John ''Cowboy'' Kissinger, his personal send-off for the money. Any other time and Bolan would have allowed a tight smile. If it went by the numbers Kissinger's artwork would be the last thing Becker saw.

Or so went the plan.

Any number of things could go wrong and Brognola had already been quick to point out just a few. The big Fed stood behind his desk, watching as his agents kept bringing in the sacks of money. When the agents brought in the final load, Brognola dismissed them, told them to shut the door on the way out.

Bolan began dumping the stacks of hundreds into the pouch. The ink was barely dried on a number of stacks. It was a rush job, granted, raiding banks, while keeping the presses rolling at the Bureau of Engraving and Printing. But it was understandable, and Bolan had to give the key people out there behind the scenes a mental salute. More than a few players on the home team had gone the extra mile to get it this far, Bolan knew. If there was any squawking about the money, any whining about all the red tape that had needed cutting to get the ransom together, Bolan hadn't heard about it. There was, indeed, something to be said, he concluded, about Americans pulling together in a crisis, coming through when their backs were to the wall.

It was far from being a done deal, of course, but Bolan wasn't going in planning to disappoint all concerned.

The Executioner heard the rotor wash of the Blackhawk chopper beyond the hole in Brognola's office. Jack Grimaldi, Stony Man Farm's number one pilot, was unavailable. He was overseas on a mission with Phoenix Force. Two blacksuit pilots from the Farm waited in the helicopter out on the street. The sun was up, and Bolan figured Becker had a good four hours' worth of time to wait and worry.

"I've got to ask it again, Striker. What if Becker decides he wants to take you with him as more added insurance?"

Bolan hadn't given his friend an answer before and he couldn't think of a reassuring one now either. "It's been a crapshoot since I first walked in there."

"Dammit, Striker, I hate to even think of it happening—you might have to go down with the ship."

"I'll try to avoid that."

Brognola frowned, but let it go. Every time Bolan headed into the killing fields they both knew and accepted the grim reality he may not return.

Brognola shifted direction away from the doom talk. "The President is pleased, to say the least, you got the bastards out of there and the hostages released. So far we're covered on our end, but it goes without saying we've got far graver things still on the plate."

Bolan gave that piece of news a nod. Because the media hadn't been allowed anywhere near the museum, and since Bolan had used another name on the spot, the Stony Man cover appeared intact. All along it had been, for the most part, the least of their concerns. Still the Stony Man cover needed to stay in the dark if it was to survive.

Currently there were countless innocent lives, snuffed out by fanatics' rage and twisted ideals and the greed of a few men, that needed to be accounted for.

"The bastards took the place cleanly, though, from the looks of it. Those security guards never stood a chance. They didn't stop there."

"I just gave Becker what he wanted all along," Bolan said, dumping more money into the pouch. "He didn't want to hold the museum any longer than he had to. He just wanted his money and to fly on."

"Well, he's flown. All of two hundred miles southwest. The E-3 Sentry/AWACS nailed them in a valley of the Blue Ridge Mountains. Damn near ironic, if you ask me. Close enough to the Farm I moved in a team of blacksuit snipers by van like you asked. They'll be ready and waiting when you get there."

"I'll smoke over the satellite pictures and iron out the particulars while I fly."

The money was loaded. Bolan zipped it up.

"There's the question of the missing ADM," Brognola said. "The word's been passed. I've got all available law enforcement, local, state and federal, and all branches of the military combing the city now, looking for any suspicious stragglers Becker may have left behind, like that Butcher. Aerial recon, door-to-door searches, you name it, we have to find that ADM."

Bolan had been thinking about Becker's last ace. "It's just a hunch, but an ADM is primarily used as a last resort."

"I'd say Becker sure has one. What are you saying?"

"Run down all real estate transactions in the outlying suburbs and the city. Start six months back and move forward. But I'm thinking Becker put it close to town. An ADM is pretty much meant to knock out railroads, airfields, bridges."

"Bridges?"

"Get some SEALs here."

The Executioner lifted the pouch. He looked at

his friend for a long moment and read the fear in Brognola's eyes.

"Get out of here, Striker. And nail these bastards."

Bolan nodded and left.

It was time to deliver.

THEY WERE stretching their legs. Both the Arabs and his own men were moving around the grounded jets, everyone searching the skies, the field, the wooded hills, waiting. Feeling the jittery nerves all around him, Ian Becker couldn't stand still. He was clock-watching, eyeing the wooded hills himself, wondering why he was suddenly so troubled. Vinyard was at his side, and Becker saw the anxiety and doubt harden on the Sergeant's face like a plaster mold. A satellite dish had been set up in front of the three jets in order to further the range of their radar. So far nothing was moving on the pilots' screens. Maybe it was nerves, maybe it was the waiting, but something didn't feel right to Becker.

"You never said, Colonel. Where to from here?"

They stood away from the jets, the sun rising over the big field in the valley. It was going to be a hot day, and already Becker was sweating. Where the hell was Belasko with his money? He had the map, he had the frequency to the pilot. No word that he was even on the way.

"We're headed to Brazil. I'm unloading some of the cash to a cleaner there. He'll take us all to Rio, and from there we board a freighter—merchant marine it all the way to Tunisia. I know, from here on it gets even more shaky. At some point I'll have to force them to take their eyes out of the sky.''

''Sir, if I can say something?''

''Speak.''

''I've got a bad gut feeling. They handed over the money too quick and easy.''

''They had no choice.'' Becker fired up a smoke, hoping it would help get his nerves together.

''Their messenger service, sir.''

''Belasko?''

''Yes, sir. I feel, with all due respect, Colonel, he played us.''

Becker felt the anger rise from his belly, his pulse racing.

''Sir, I heard the Arabs ask you about their cut. I heard them want to know how you plan to evac their own. And what about Max Kelly?''

''It's in the works. That's just one reason Sampson is staying behind. I'll address all concerns once we collect the rest of our money and are out of the country.'' Becker gave Vinyard a cold look. ''Anything else, Sergeant?''

''It's your show, Colonel.''

''That it is, Sergeant. What's to worry? We've got the nukes. The President thinks we've got anthrax ready to blow from a rooftop over the city. The excitement we created has got all available resources back there tied up. As for Belasko, he's just what you said—the President's errand boy. They wanted us gone and the only way to do that was to pay us.

I hope I don't see or hear any more doubt again, Sergeant. Am I clear?''

Vinyard clenched his jaws. "Yes, sir."

The pilot's voice suddenly patched through. Becker grabbed his handheld radio, then pitched away his cigarette. "What have you got?"

"A lone bird, Colonel, coming in from the north. Belasko just radioed. I cleared him for a landing."

Becker smiled at Vinyard. "You know I just thought of something, Sergeant. A billion dollars cash, cleaned up and ready to be spent: that kind of money has to be the next best thing to eternal life."

17

Five of Becker's finest, Bolan saw, were marching away from the C-20s across the open field as the Blackhawk touched down. Their MP-5s in hand, they picked up the pace to a jog. Bolan could be sure they were poised to cut loose at the first sign this wasn't a straight delivery. No sweat. This was one play the Executioner wasn't about to let them call.

The Farm had torn a page out of Becker's manual. When clearing the hills for landing, Bolan had sent the blacksuits the vibrating signal from his pager. They sent back their own vibrating signal moments later to let the soldier know they were good to go on their end. On Bolan's order the blacksuit pilots had put down the chopper at the west edge of the field. Becker's troops would have to leg it a good hundred meters to reach the Blackhawk.

Bolan already had the door open, the pouches lined up near the edge, ready for easy pickup. Waiting for the enemy to arrive, the Executioner took in the stage for final delivery. The terrorist army was strung out but packed tightly down the port side of the closest C-20, the other two jets grounded just beyond its stern. The aircraft were aligned in a staggered formation. Recalling the enemy numbers he'd seen walk from the museum, they all looked to be front and center. Bolan couldn't have asked for a better set-up for his surprise send-off.

Like Becker, he was going for broke here, all or nothing.

They greeted Bolan with laughing eyes as they hunched, forging into the rotor wash. The Executioner recognized them all from their military jackets. Vinyard, Biltman, Artillon, Weathers and Kurchin. For a moment he was tempted to wonder where and why it had all gone so wrong for what were once brave and supremely talented American fighting men but who had tossed it all away. And for what? Money? A chip on the shoulder that the world had moved beyond them? Some grandiose, in-your-face statement to carve their place in history? He gave it no more than another moment's fleeting reflection. They were what they had become—savages, no more, no less.

"Shut it down!" Biltman shouted at Bolan.

Bolan passed the word to the pilots. Twin GE turbo shafts were killed, the dust storm beginning to thin moments later.

"Glad you could make the party, Belasko," Biltman said, and laughed. "We were getting worried you wouldn't show. We'd hate to cause anymore unnecessary grief back in town, you understand. I'm sure they want to get back to work on the Hill, pass out a bunch of tough new anti-terrorist laws. Assholes that they are.''

Bolan held Biltman's laughing stare. "Let's get on with it.''

They started hauling out the pouches. Biltman reached for the delivery bag by Bolan's leg but the Executioner was already picking it up. He looked up at Bolan, smiling. The look vanished when he gave Bolan's side arms a steely once-over. He radioed Becker.

"Colonel, our errand boy here is armed.''

"What's he going to do? Arrest us? Shoot us each in the head? Leave it.''

"Tell Becker I'm walking the last bag in with you.''

"I heard that, Biltman. Come on, Belasko. But, just remember I've still got the power. We get the money, you get your city back. ''

Bag in hand, the Executioner disembarked from the Blackhawk. It was time to roll the doomsday dice.

THEY BEGAN transferring the money from the pouches to large burlap sacks. The tension thickened, and Bolan could feel the adrenaline surge all around. The sight of all that money looked to anger a few of the Arabs. Becker laughed at their suspicion, then tossed a few stacks to his Islamic cronies, as if to appease them.

"There's more where that came from, gentlemen. It's payday, people.''

Bolan held onto the last pouch while they laughed and congratulated one another, grabbing loot, a couple of them even kissing a few stacks.

"Land of opportunity," the shaved-head Kurchin chuckled. "It's what makes America so great."

"I love this country, brother!" Weathers chimed in. "America the beautiful!"

"Stifle all that noise. Keep moving." Becker got on his handheld. "Magruder, how are we looking?"

"Nothing on the screens, sir. So far, so good. Looks like you made them true believers."

"Keep me posted. And don't fire up those engines until I give the word. I don't want to spend the day chasing money all over this field. Copy that."

"That's a roger, sir."

"Out." He looked at Bolan. "Just remember, in case the President gives the order to send some fighter jets to escort us out of the country, I can set off those three nukes anywhere, anytime. And don't forget the anthrax."

"You're in complete control, Becker."

Becker nodded at the last pouch. "You want to give that up now, Belasko? Or maybe you want a little piece of the action?" he laughed.

Bolan played along. "Not enough there to cover the time and trouble. I'll pass."

Becker didn't know how to take that, but laughed anyway. It was his moment to shine.

Then Bolan saw a few of Becker's soldiers scanning the hills and the skies through field glasses, and felt the tension tighten in his chest. The blacksuits

were ordered to stay hidden, but Bolan wasn't about
to give it up to chance they wouldn't be spotted.
Either way he was ready to make his move, even if
it meant handing Brognola his worst fear.

"How are we looking out there, gentlemen?"

"Clean, sir."

"Outstanding. The bag, Belasko."

Bolan set the bag down beside Becker. "If that's
all...."

The colonel zipped open the bag and began taking
out bills. "What's your hurry? Stay awhile, let's
have a few laughs. I've got some whiskey onboard.
How about a drink to celebrate?"

Bolan showed Becker an easy smile. The man
smelled something, but wasn't sure what.

"I'll pass again. Have a nice trip."

He felt Becker measure him with a long stare.

"Just going to run off? That's kind of rude,"
Becker said, but laughed.

There was no other way than to brazen it out.
Turning, Bolan began heading back for the chopper.
Out of the corner of his eye, he saw Becker still
watching him.

"Hey, Belasko!"

Bolan looked back, but kept moving away. Having seen them in action, he kept waiting for them to
open fire. The bullets never came.

"It's been a pleasure doing business with you."

Bolan said nothing but thought the pleasure was
about to be all his.

BECKER WAS digging out the last few stacks. He was light-headed with euphoria. He still couldn't believe it was actually happening. The radar screens were clear of air traffic, the money just about sacked up. Morale was high; even the sulking Arabs were now lightening up some, counting a piece of their cut, with visions of carrying the future torch for their jihad.

A billion dollars in cash. They had won, the dream come true. The opposition had given in, groveling before him like whipped puppies the whole time. Not that they ever stood a chance to keep him from getting what he wanted, so richly deserved, but he had expected at least some threat of retaliation.

All was bliss. Brazil, Tunisia, then his big contact, a drug lord in Burma waiting with open arms. Jungle refuge for awhile, once they got to the other end, just like the old days. The future was wide open to all kinds of possibilities, the proverbial sky's the limit.

He *was* God, after all, Becker decided. They had risen from the dead. They had left their mark, forever changing how every man, woman and child saw the United States government.

Outstanding.

He was grabbing up money as fast as he could, thinking life couldn't get any sweeter when he noticed it.

"What the hell?"

Becker looked up and saw Belasko walking toward the Blackhawk. Looking down again to make sure he wasn't seeing things in his buzz of joy, he stared at the bottom of the pouch. It had to be a joke, but something warned him it wasn't.

Becker felt his blood run cold. For some reason the pouch didn't seem to settle on the ground right either, certainly not flat. He gave it a lift. It was empty now, but it was way too damn heavy. Then he saw it, and felt the first wave of sickness churn his gut. Either by accident or design they had left part of the detonator cord sticking out, lying at the bottom of the pouch.

Becker saw the world spin, followed by a rush of noise in his ears, a terrible ringing of rage and terror that erupted from his heart. He looked up, fumbled in his pants pocket for the big box, when he spotted Belasko just standing there, staring at him from across the field. He thought he actually spotted a smile on the treacherous bastard's lips, thought he even heard Belasko call out something to the effect, "Have a nice flight."

The curse rolled up with the taste of bile in Becker's throat as he saw Belasko raise a small object in his hand and point his way.

"Belasko! You fu—"

BOLAN DIDN'T let Becker finish.

"Have a nice flight," the Executioner repeated as he hit the doomsday button to fling all their sick ambition and dreams of terror back in their faces.

The thunderclap shattered the silence across the valley; the fireball blowing with hurricane force through the terrorist horde. The lead jet was pulverized to scrap while the fire reached out, hungry for more destruction. The blast and shock wave hammered the other two C-20s, lifting them off their wheels, pinning them together for the blink of an eye before the wings sheared off, flesh and metal bonding, and were hurled far out across the field as their own fuel tanks ignited in a momentarily stunning flash.

There were runners, several dozen at first glance, but Bolan had already anticipated survivors going rabbit. Right before he blew their world apart, he saw enemy numbers breaking in flight, aware something was about to go terribly wrong, hardmen scrambling to save their doomed worlds.

The blacksuits went to work even before the first body hit the earth. From the woods above and behind Bolan they cut loose with their weapons. Out there on the hellground, armed figures were dashing in all directions or hauling themselves up after hasty nosedives. The blacksuits, ten in all, Bolan knew, had brought a mixed bag of firepower. A few Remington 700 sniper rifles began locking onto the terrorists, 7.62 mm lead scoring several quick head shots. A few AR-18 assault rifles began stammering out in-sync with the big sniper pieces, those blacksuits giving a few more runners some lead before dropping them in the outer limits of fire and raining debris.

Thunder pealed on and on, as fireballs began marching through the flaming scrap and smoky perimeter. Bodies took to the air, shredded beyond human recognition. The remaining blacksuits kept laying down the blanket of explosives, chugged fiery doom out from their compact H&K-69 grenade launchers, then pumping still more 40 mm grenades into the blazing scrap heaps, driving further home the message no one out there was leaving in one piece.

They were busy clearing the way for the Executioner to mop up any stragglers or wounded. The bad always die hard and angry, not wanting to give it up until the last breath was crushed out of them. Bolan didn't think past experience would prove him wrong this time.

Bolan hopped into the Blackhawk and grabbed his M-16/M-203 combo from an aft compartment in the chopper. The M-203's breech was already filled with a 40 mm grenade, the assault rifle's clip full.

Locked and loaded, Bolan slipped the satchel of grenades and spare clips over his shoulder. He let the blacksuits continue for a few more seconds, then decided the up close and personal touch was the only solid option to see it finished.

The Executioner unclipped his handheld and radioed the blacksuit team leader as he leapt out the doorway.

"Striker to Anvil Watch, come in."

"Anvil Watch here, Striker."

"Hold your fire, but cover me. I'm going in."

"That's affirmative, Striker. Anvil Watch has your back."

It was Bolan's task to close it out.

The Executioner surged ahead, M-16 fanning the flames. He was closing, a dozen or so yards out, when his first targets reared up. They were reeling beyond the fire, bloodied and groaning, holding hard to weapons. Two SMGs flamed short bursts, the slugs gouging divots beside his feet, when Bolan drilled them in the chest with a 5.56 mm sweep that knocked them off their feet.

Burning gas, blood and bodily waste pierced Bolan's senses as he stepped past the sprawled bodies. Flames reached out, kissing Bolan's face with scorching fury. Money, torched and flying everywhere, floated past the soldier or was sucked into the fire.

The Executioner rolled on.

Three more gunners came into sight as they beat a weaving path from the inferno at twelve o'clock. Bolan hosed them down, a straight line of slugs tearing across their backs to send them pitching in boneless sprawls.

He scanned the carnage. He saw a limb twitch out for an MP-5. A black wall of smoke cloaked the figure as it shuddered to its feet, minus an arm. Bolan rolled through the veil, his senses choked. Dead ahead, he met two white orbs, the eyes behind the scarlet veil fired with pain and hate. Bolan recognized Daniel Biltman.

The Executioner brought the assault rifle up, held down the M-16's trigger and gave the one-armed Biltman a last taste of rage on his way to hell.

Scanning, Bolan reached into his satchel, drew and cracked home a fresh clip. He was well beyond the ring of fire when he spotted the mangled remains of two terrorists crabbing and moaning along. One hardman had no legs, the other tying a one-handed suture to hold back his guts. A quick mercy burst from Bolan pinned them where they crawled.

It looked like a wrap, but the Executioner gave the kill zone a long look and walk-through, just in case.

Nothing but the dead stretched before the Executioner.

Bolan raised his blacksuit leader as flaming bills fluttered past his sight. "We're through here. Take it on home."

The Executioner caught the affirmative on the other end but he was already moving away from the slaughter.

Unless Bolan missed his guess, there was still some hunting left.

18

"Mother Nature gave up number three, Striker. How do you like that for one last kick in the teeth for Becker?"

Bolan was in the Blackhawk when he got the news from Brognola over the sat-link. The chopper had landed at Stony Man Farm for refueling, then Bolan passed the order on to the pilots to get him back to Washington. They were airborne once again.

After neutralizing the terrorist force Bolan had reported back to Brognola, told the big Fed Becker and company were no longer a problem.

Brognola sounded almost normal again to Bolan, the edge of fear and anger gone from his voice. "A police river patrol spotted the third ADM. It was secured to a middle pillar on Key Bridge. If Becker had set it off, Striker, do you know it would have taken out most of Georgetown on one side and most of Rosslyn on the other. Kurtzman ran down the potential damage on his computer, using the blast yield and other factors, including radioactive fallout. The Bear did it for future reference in case, God forbid, we come across one of these again. The loss of life and property would have been staggering."

"It worked out."

"On the President's end it's a mess. The loss of innocent life...I wouldn't want to be in his shoes. The fact that Becker and his terrorist army were neutralized, well, I don't think any amount of vengeance would be consolation enough for the victims. He's addressing the nation sometime today."

"And the ADM?"

"There's a SEAL unit on the Potomac now. You know, Becker factored in people, places and things, but he didn't count on Mother Nature giving him the final middle-finger salute. Due to the scorching heat, the Potomac's been dropping a foot-and-a-half to three feet a day the past week. We haven't had rain for several weeks. Highly unusual this time of year. Beyond that, I can't even remember the last time this town saw a decent rainfall. At any rate, they didn't secure the ADM deep enough."

"It happens. They're history. What's the story on the senators?"

"I ran that by the President like you wanted. Since there's no longer a Becker or an ADM to consider, he wants to turn the situation over to a Rapid Response Team. Fort Bragg has already flown them in."

"The opposition has made no contact?"

"None. But since you've come this far the President was wondering if you had a plan?"

Bolan did and gave it Brognola.

MAX KELLY listened to the news again, his heart thumping with mounting anger.

"The hostages were released before dawn, that much we know, but no one official, either from the Army, the police or the FBI, is letting us speak with any of the hostages at this time. Now we've heard that three military jets flew right off the Mall following the release of the hostages, and we have an unconfirmed report the terrorists had boarded the aircraft—"

Kelly snapped off the television. He'd heard more than enough to confirm a nagging suspicion. He was supposed to receive contact from Sampson, along with instructions on how to proceed, three hours after Becker had released control of the museum and flew. Nine hours and counting if he believed the news that they had flown before dawn. Still no Sampson. It felt wrong. Suddenly he lost faith in the Colonel. It occurred to him, as he felt the blood pressure roar into his ears, that maybe he had been chosen as Becker's human sacrifice.

If that was the case...

Uzi subgun in hand, Kelly was moving into the den off the hallway, feeling mean and angry, when the object crashed through the window. The tear gas canister hissed but Kelly bolted out of the den before the cloud choked his senses.

All hell was suddenly breaking loose. Kelly had no choice but to save himself. He knew it was useless, as the armored and black-helmeted commandos stormed the place, from all directions it seemed. But he was a soldier, proud and fearless, and was going out with a roar.

Kelly caught a glimpse of Senator Walker charging one of the Arabs. Walker was a blur in the living room as Kelly bulldozed into the Arab who was swinging his submachine gun, looking as if he hoped to line up the ex-Marine's family for a clean sweep. The Arab appeared to hesitate at the sight of the commandos coming up from the basement, down the steps from upstairs, into the living room from the kitchen, their own MP-5 SMGs locked and already spraying lead. There was screaming from the living room, a bellow of rage from the war hero as Walker launched the Arab into the bay window with so much force the heavy glass shattered.

Kelly roared, all fury and despair, went for it even as the front door behind him blew open to the charge of still more commandos. He was cutting loose on the first two commandos in sight, holding down the trigger of his MP-5. He had a fleeting vision of Becker out there, somewhere in the world, counting his billion, laughing all the way to his cleaners, when everything went black.

THE EXECUTIONER was in position at the back of the house, settling in at the edge of the deck. His blacksuit teams were ready, waiting for the order to storm the house. When the word was sent, commando teams would storm both kidnap sites. A simultaneous attack.

Bolan listened to the silence, counting off the doomsday numbers. He heard some shouting and cursing beyond the sliding glass door. It was just the distraction he needed to blow his way in.

He paused, gave the setup a moment's reflection. The Blackhawk had set down on a street, well away from the perimeter of Senator Spellman's private property. With his M-16 set on fullauto, the soldier had jogged in the rest of the way. The blacksuits were currently out front, armed and waiting for anything Bolan might flush their way.

He had no fix on numbers, going in blind, but he was ready for a full charge. He was about to slip on his gas mask and prime the tear gas canister when he heard shooting erupt inside the house.

The Executioner blew in the glass with a burst of M-16 autofire and charged through, clearing the shards by inches. Something had gone terribly wrong among the terrorists. Maybe it was frayed nerves, or a doomed feeling Becker was going to leave them behind.

Whatever had happened, one of them had snapped, leaving Bolan with two less terrorists to take out, he discovered on his way in. Beyond the rattle of autofire and the distinct chugging of a sound-suppressed pistol, Bolan caught the screaming of the man and woman in the far corner of the living room. They ducked out of sight, falling for cover behind a large couch.

A big hardman holding turf in a doorway was pouring it on with a mini-Uzi, firing across the living room, when he noticed the invader too late.

Bolan cut him down, a line of 5.56 mm slugs

chopping his torso to red ruins, flinging him out of sight. The Executioner set his sights on a woman behind the wet bar. She was a whirl of frenzied movement in the corner of his eye, firing away with her pistol, driving the soldier to cover. There was the distant stutter of weapons' fire, a loud crash, and Bolan knew the blacksuits were inside.

Bolan ducked, hitting the edge of the kitchen corner as bullets gouged hunks of drywall.

"Give it up," Bolan told the blonde.

She cursed in a foreign tongue Bolan didn't recognize. He steeled himself, glancing at the two bodies on the carpet. He added up the scene here. Whoever she was she had panicked and shot two of the terrorists in the back of the heads. Only the big one was a little too quick and beat it to cover before she could nail him.

She began to fire at Bolan, leaving the Executioner no choice. He wheeled around the corner and drilled a burst into her chest. She folded, a look of profound bewilderment on her face, before dropping from sight behind the wet bar. Bolan saw the blacksuits, crouched and moving down the hall beyond the living room, their M-16s fanning in all directions.

"Senator Spellman?"

"Y-y-yes, yes."

"Are you or your wife hit?"

"No."

"Are they any others in the house?"

"No."

Bolan moved away from the wall, told the black-suits, "We're clear."

The senator crawled a few feet beyond the couch on his knees. At first, Bolan thought the man was injured, then the Senator clambered up on shaking legs. He wondered why Spellman didn't go to his wife, give her a hug or some words of comfort. There was a look in her eyes, as she lifted herself from behind the couch, that warned Bolan something more had happened here. Whatever it was it wasn't his problem.

The Executioner watched a trembling Senator Spellman make himself a drink. Bolan put them out of mind, took his handheld, and raised the commanding officer on the other end.

"Prong One to Prong Two. Come in, Prong Two."

"Prong Two here. Situation under control on this end. Bad guys neutralized. Hostages are all accounted for, no harm done to any friendlies."

"Likewise, I'm clear on this end," Bolan said. "Prong Two over and out."

The Executioner gave the senator and his wife one last curious look.

Spellman killed his drink and looked at Bolan. "Whoever you are, thank you. Thank God you showed up when you did. She went berserk, just start shooting. She would have killed us if you hadn't showed when you did."

The wife spoke up from the couch, pinning her

husband with a look that would have scared the devil. "Your problems have only just begun."

For some reason, the Executioner believed that. On the way out, Bolan told the blacksuits to make sure they rounded up all discarded weapons.

Take
2 explosive books
plus a
mystery bonus
FREE

JAMES AXLER

DEATHLANDS®

Shadow World

Ryan Cawdor must face the threat of invaders that arrive from a parallel earth where the nukecaust never happened. And when he is abducted through a time corridor, he discovers a nightmare that makes Deathlands look tame by comparison!

On sale March 2000 at your favorite retail outlet. Or order your copy now by sending your name, address, zip or postal code, along with a check or money order (please do not send cash) for $5.99 for each book ordered ($6.99 in Canada), plus 75¢ postage and handling ($1.00 in Canada), payable to Gold Eagle Books, to:

In the U.S.	In Canada
Gold Eagle Books	Gold Eagle Books
3010 Walden Ave.	P.O. Box 636
P.O. Box 9077	Fort Erie, Ontario
Buffalo, NY 14269-9077	L2A 5X3

Please specify book title with order.
Canadian residents add applicable federal and provincial taxes.

GOLD EAGLE®

GDL49

JAMES AXLER

DEATH LANDS®

Pandora's Redoubt

Ryan Cawdor and his fellow survivalists emerge in a redoubt in which they discover a sleek superarmored personnel carrier bristling with weapons from predark days. As the companions leave the redoubt, a sudden beeping makes them realize why the builders were constructing a supermachine in the first place.